THE ELECTION CONNECTION

MONICA TILLERY

Author of *The Confection Connection* and *A Sweet Deal*

CRIMSON
ROMANCE
F+W Media, Inc.

Published by
Crimson Romance
an imprint of F+W Media, Inc.
10151 Carver Road, Suite 200
Blue Ash, OH 45242. U.S.A.
www.crimsonromance.com

ISBN 10: 1-4405-9066-4
ISBN 13: 978-1-4405-9066-5
eISBN 10: 1-4405-9067-2
eISBN 13: 978-1-4405-9067-2

This is a work of fiction. Names, characters, corporations, institutions, organizations, events, or locales in this novel are either the product of the author's imagination or, if real, used fictitiously. The resemblance of any character to actual persons (living or dead) is entirely coincidental.

*For our beautiful cousin, Ashley Tillery Weeks,
in honor of your sacrifice, and in loving memory of
Army Specialist Ari Daniel Brown-Weeks
1984-2007
Forever in our hearts*

Acknowledgments

No matter what I write, it's always better after my wonderful editor, Jess Verdi, gets her hands on it. Thank you for another amazing job! It was fun and gratifying to work with you, as always, and I can't wait to do it again.

Thank you also to Tara Gelsomino for believing in me and my book. I truly love working with you and look forward to a bright future together.

As always, thank you to my wonderful husband, Dave, for your unwavering support and enthusiasm. You are awesome.

Chapter One

Lily Ashton took Congressman Ford Richardson's offered hand and pulled herself out of the Town Car, careful not to scuff her Louboutins on the pavement or flash her panties to the paparazzi. Ford kissed her temple before waving to the crowd and flashing his best campaign smile. As usual, she played it up, gazing at him in adoration for the cameras, though to be honest, it wasn't much of a chore. His thick, dark hair, strong jaw, and polished good looks were easy on the eyes. He wore a suit like nobody's business, but they hadn't been dating quite long enough for her to know what was beneath those expensive fabrics. She had a good idea, though, and the warm, muscled skin she felt beneath her hands when she slipped her arm around his waist during fundraisers and cocktail parties told her she was in for quite a treat if things ever went that far.

They hurried past the onlookers, tossing out smiles and waves, but no comments, until they reached the hotel where her best friend's wedding reception would be held. Once they were safely inside the posh lobby, Ford slowed his stride and took her hand. Her heels clicked against the mirror-smooth marble floors, and the rush of guests traveling through the space moved the hotel's signature lemon-coconut scent over them in a fragrant breeze.

"Thank you for that." He always softened when they were alone, turning off the public persona and becoming more human and less politician.

"For what?" She smoothed her hair and took in the details of the gorgeous hotel lobby. From the impeccably dressed hotel employees to the sophisticated décor, every aspect of the space screamed elegant decadence.

"For the pictures out there. This is Carly's day, not mine. I wish we could just go out sometimes and not have photographers waiting outside." He'd leaned close enough for her to feel the warmth of his breath on her neck and catch a hint of his sophisticated scent.

If he thought any of the paparazzi outside had come to catch a glimpse of him, then the campaign had scrambled his brain. Carly and her new husband, Michael, were both amazing bakers who met as rival contestants on a reality baking show but ended up falling in love last year when they teamed up to work on a celebrity wedding. Their popularity exploded when they joined forces to create a show on the Cuisine Network where they traveled the world, putting their own spin on popular tourist attractions with inventive themed cakes. Viewers were rewarded with a romantic proposal on the last episode of the season, and the big day had finally come. They had made a slew of famous friends through the show and in working on high-profile weddings. Their reception was going to be teeming with A-listers from every facet of entertainment.

"We can, but maybe not to the wedding of two television stars who have a ton of famous friends. I'm sure half the paparazzi don't even know who they're waiting for, and you just got some free publicity, Congressman. You're welcome." Cameras did follow Ford much of the time they went out, but sometimes she wondered if he didn't enjoy the attention a little more than he let on.

With a gentle hand at her elbow, he led her into the reception, and she stood in awe of her friend's glamorous dream made reality. Lily had worked closely with Carly during every step of the wedding and reception planning, but seeing it all come together was breathtaking. The hotel was spectacular, but the decorated ballroom was almost unbelievable. Soft pinks, creamy ivories, and stark blacks mingled in the fabrics, their wedding cake, the china, and linens. It was gorgeous, but weddings were always bittersweet for her.

She felt mentally healthy enough to be genuinely happy for her friend, though, and watching the pair say their vows earlier was magical. Lily was ready to celebrate them now. The newly married couple bustled into the lobby and stood outside the ballroom doors, waiting for the emcee to announce their arrival, so there was no time for self-pity. She exchanged elated grins with Carly and watched as they drifted in, the crowd parting for them, and walked to the dance floor.

"Please welcome, for the first time, Mr. and Mrs. Michael Welch!" the DJ's voice boomed through the speakers. Wild applause and cheers drowned out the first strains of Stevie Wonder's "For Once in my Life" as they moved to the center of the dance floor to share their first dance as husband and wife. Michael gazed down at Carly as he held her in his arms, his expression one of a man completely and utterly consumed by love. Lily couldn't hear what they murmured to one another, but she knew it was sweet. It was amazing to see her friend find someone so perfect for her.

Ford pulled Lily close, and she laid her head on his shoulder as they watched Carly dance with her new husband. A lump formed in her throat, and she swiped a single tear from under her lashes, determined not to make a mess of her makeup tonight. How many first dances would she watch before her first thought wasn't of Nathan? Ford kissed the top of her head, and they parted to clap for the couple as the song ended. Carly had planned an elaborate sit-down dinner, so Lily and Ford wound through the crowd to the head table to take their seats. Ever the gentleman, he pulled her chair out for her and helped her push it under the table before chatting with the other wedding party members.

Carly and Michael arrived at the table, flushed with happiness, and took their seats in the middle, with Carly sitting beside Lily.

Lily leaned over and gave her friend a hug. "Everything looks absolutely perfect, Mrs. Welch." Carly's huge grin was proof that she was over the moon. "Be sure to eat at least a little of every course before you get back out there and circulate. You won't get another chance once you leave this table."

"That shouldn't be a problem. I'm starving." Carly sat back and accepted her salad from the uniformed waiter. Laughing the whole time, she let Michael feed her a forkful of leafy greens.

Courses came and went on exquisite china: there was a green salad, creamy tomato bisque, filet mignon paired with asparagus tips and herbed potatoes, and finally an elegant scoop of perfectly smooth lemon sorbet. Lily indulged herself in the decadent meal, just this once. She'd been blessed with the fast metabolism that made it possible for her to eat like a normal person while building a career in modeling, but she knew better than to push her luck. At twenty-seven, a slower metabolism could be lurking around the corner, waiting to knock her out of modeling and into something that would make her glad she'd gone ahead and finished college. Transitioning to full-time work at Soldier On was something she wanted to do on her own timeline rather than be forced into it because she needed a job.

A waiter swept by the table, giving every guest a cut crystal flute of bubbly, and Lily reviewed her maid of honor toast in her head. She'd promised herself she wouldn't cry, wouldn't say anything stupid, and wouldn't embarrass the congressman. She wasn't technically his girlfriend, but when they were on dates she responded to an unspoken pressure to present herself a certain way.

She looked out into the sea of faces, seeing familiar friends and family interspersed with celebrities from music and television and plenty of industry professionals from Michael and Carly's life she had never met. Lily didn't care about connections one way or the other, but Ford was likely drooling from the possibilities. Celebrity endorsements would be like gold for his re-election campaign.

She stood to give her speech, eyes already welling up before she'd uttered a single word. So much for not getting too emotional.

Carly was the best person she knew, and no words could do their friendship justice, but she'd try. Dozens of hours spent at her laptop had finally resulted in a speech that conveyed at least some of the immense love and gratitude she had for her best friend.

"Carly and Michael, my heart is so full for you today. America watched you fall in love on television, and the real thing is just as beautiful as what they saw on screen." She took a deep breath to steady her nerves before continuing, and Carly took her hand.

"Carly, I'll never forget the day we met, in ninth grade biology class. You were already great with a knife, and I was well on my way to relying on you to catch me when I fall. I know you weren't expecting your lab partner to faint beside you, but I was so glad you were there. And you've been there for me ever since.

"Michael, I know that if Carly chose you, then you must be someone very special. Carly deserves the very best of everything in life, and for her, you're just that." Her voice caught in her throat as Michael draped his arm over Carly's shoulder and pulled her closer. "I know that the rest of your life together will be as beautiful as today has been, and I wish you nothing but happiness. Finding your one perfect match is a rare gift, and I'm so glad it happened to you two. Congratulations."

She raised her glass and sipped her champagne, swallowing past the lump in her throat. Carly's eyes shone with tears as she stood and took Lily's hand. "Thank you, Lil. That was beautiful."

"I love you guys so much." Lily pushed the words out. Perhaps she should have left the part about how rare the perfect match was. Sometimes she wondered if she'd ever be able to let go of Nathan and find love again. Most of the time, she didn't even want to try. Michael stood and leaned over to kiss her cheek, and Lily gave Carly a hug before handing over the microphone to the best man for his decidedly less emotional speech. It felt great to laugh along with his jokes and let the emotional weight lift from her shoulders.

Ford's hand found her knee under the table when she took her seat, and he squeezed. Leaning against him, she enjoyed the strength of his solid frame. His familiar black pepper and cinnamon scent drifted over her in a ribbon of warmth as he dipped his head to whisper in her ear as the best man concluded his toast.

"Can we dance? Or do I need to wait a little longer before I get you all to myself?" His thumb traced a lazy circle against her knee.

She turned into him, shivering a little at the light brush of his stubble against her cheek. "I'd love to dance." With her maid of honor duties complete for the time being, she was free to enjoy her handsome date.

Ford took her hand and led her through the crowd on the dance floor, cutting through without hesitation. The song ended as they found their spot, and "Dream a Little Dream of Me" spilled from the speakers, the sultry love song winding around them as he pulled her into his arms.

"Did I mention how gorgeous you look tonight?" Ford's breath was gentle against her skin, softly flowing across her neck.

She dipped her chin and gazed up at him through lowered lashes. "Yes, but I don't mind if you say it again."

Lily closed the gap between them and laid her head on his shoulder, enjoying the weight of his chin against the top of her head. They moved effortlessly, as though they'd danced together a thousand times, and her eyes drifted closed. He was strong, solid, beneath her touch, and for the few moments they were on the dance floor, she let herself forget that she'd ever been broken by loss. In Ford's arms there was comfort, as temporary as it may be. She knew the weekend of nonstop wedding activities was making her sappy and romantic, that she and Ford weren't moving forward, but it was fun while they were there. As the song ended, they stepped apart, and he kissed her forehead. A popular ballad began, and he pulled her back into his arms for another slow dance.

"You know, this is really nice. We should dance more often." His voice rumbled beneath her cheek, and she smiled. He was the perfect height, and they had a natural rhythm together that couldn't be denied.

Lily leaned back to look into Ford's eyes, the piercing blue enchanting her, and agreed. "I think you're right. You should invite me to more fancy parties before you head back to D.C."

"I knew I loved coming home during our recesses for a reason." He pulled her closer and hummed as they swayed together. Manufactured romantic feelings or not, being in Ford's arms felt right.

The sultry music ended, and the DJ's voice cut through the noisy crowd. "You know what time it is! All the single ladies, please come to the dance floor. The beautiful bride is ready for the bouquet toss." The single female guests flooded onto the dance floor as the men headed for the sidelines, and Lily grumbled. At least Carly had nixed Michael's idea to have "Single Ladies" play during the stampede. The last thing she wanted to do was scramble for the bouquet with the other unmarried women, but she wouldn't ruin her friend's fun.

She'd married Nathan after a whirlwind courtship, barely catching her breath between the heady early days of infatuation and their simple wedding she'd thrown together with her best friend Carly. They'd been young and impulsive, but they were perfect together, and she'd never felt that with anyone else. It was irrational, but trying to find love again felt a bit like erasing the past. Her marriage had been short-lived but blissful, marred only by the rift between her and her parents that cropped up when they objected to her getting married so young. Having both experienced and lost perfect, all-consuming, life-completing love was almost too much to bear.

She dragged herself into the throng of single women and shot a quick glance at Ford, who was studying his fingernails as though there would be a test later. He seemed to be as commitment-averse as she was, and that was just fine with her. She was lucky to find a man she enjoyed that didn't push for more, so she never questioned why he was so willing to keep the distance between them. Carly stood in front of the gaggle of giggling girls and threw a devilish grin over her shoulder at Lily. *No, please no. Not me. Anyone but me.* But Carly expertly winged the bouquet directly into Lily's hands and looked so pleased with herself that Lily couldn't be angry. The flowers couldn't have weighed more than a pound, but they might as well have been a ton of bricks. She pasted a bright smile on her face and joined her best friend for a picture of her raising the bouquet while they linked arms. Carly meant no harm, she knew that, but she wondered if it was a subtle hint that it was time to move on and find a husband. Again.

• • •

Guests lined the walkway that ran from the hotel to the couple's waiting limousine, faces glowing from the happy occasion and generous amounts of premium alcohol. Ford watched Lily in the moonlight, still surprised at her seemingly effortless beauty, as she waited for her friend to rush by through a cloud of bubbles and well wishes. Even after a full day of maid of honor duties, the wedding, and the reception, she looked perfect. Still luminous, still animated, and most incredibly, still wearing those torture devices she called shoes.

He took her hand, lacing his fingers through hers, and squeezed. Her big brown eyes shined with genuine warmth when she looked up at him. He pushed a rogue tendril of chocolate brown hair behind her ear and was rewarded when she pressed her cheek against his hand, just for a second. The intimacy in that fleeting moment sent a jolt down his spine. "Thanks for inviting me. Your friends seem really happy together."

"They are." Lily looked away and took a shuddering breath. "I'm so happy for Carly. She waited a long time for her perfect man."

The couple burst through the door, hand in hand, wearing identical dazzling smiles. Their photographer and videographer hustled along the walk ahead of them, navigating the pebbled terrain as they walked backwards to capture both the reveling guests and the departing couple. Friends and family blew bubbles and shouted their congratulations as Michael and Carly made their way through the crowd, and Carly stopped by Lily to pull her into a quick, fierce hug. She whispered something in her ear while her new husband stood by, smiling fondly.

The couple disappeared into their limousine and drove off, empty soda cans rattling behind them. The crowd dispersed quickly and without much further comment as the taillights grew dim, and just like that, the party was over.

"I'm dead on my feet, but you look like you could stay up all night," Ford murmured to Lily as he texted the driver to bring their car around.

She laughed. "This is all an act; believe me, I'm completely exhausted and can't wait to kick these shoes off. This is only possible because I've had years of practice. I'll be lucky if I get out of this dress before I collapse into bed tonight."

Unbidden, thoughts of helping Lily out of her dress popped in his head, and he wondered if she was having similar thoughts. He shouldn't be reading more into his date's casual affections and wondering if something real could ever develop between them. They had a good time together, they enjoyed a spicy chemistry, but he wasn't looking for anything serious, not after what happened the one and only time he'd come close to getting engaged. If not for his mother's interference, Ford had no doubt that he'd be happily married today, probably a father several times over. At eighteen, he'd known he was ready to commit to his girlfriend before they went off to college, but Mother put a stop to it. Courtney Simons hadn't been good enough for Jessica Richardson's son, and there was no way in hell she would marry into the family. As one of the five students attending Ford's prestigious private school on financial scholarship, Courtney was little more than an opportunistic gold digger as far as Mother was concerned.

Ford hadn't yet grown his backbone and let her convince him to end the relationship, let her chase his girlfriend away while telling himself that Mother was right, he needed to concentrate on his education. Now Courtney was married to another man, someone who deserved her a hell of a lot more than he ever did, and Ford was alone. Over the years, his love for Courtney had indeed faded into fond affection, but the thought of getting close to marriage again made bile rise in this throat. He couldn't consider marriage without remembering the spineless boy who couldn't find a way to stand up for himself. Between frustration that his mother would interfere in such a way and his disgust at himself for allowing it, he'd sworn off serious relationships. Until he could look in the mirror and not see the man who'd let his mother dissuade him from marrying the woman he'd loved, he wouldn't chance it.

One of the things he enjoyed about dating Lily was that she never asked for more from him—never called first, never asked to define the relationship, never pushed for more time together. Being with someone who seemed as averse to commitment as he was freeing. Lily was perfect for him: quick-witted, polished, and stunning. They had a good time together, definitely enjoyed a mutual attraction, but she was content to keep him at arm's length, and he liked it that way. Since swearing off serious relationships and marriage, Ford found that most of his relationships didn't last very long; most women wanted their relationships to go somewhere, not continue endlessly without ever progressing. In Lily, he'd been able to enjoy everything he loved about dating without the possibility of disaster.

"If you're that tired, maybe we should get a suite here. I'd hate for you to collapse from exhaustion." He grinned and pretended to head back into the hotel. Now that he'd imagined helping her out of her dress, getting a room together seemed like a great idea. He had to stop.

"Not tonight. Take me home, Congressman. I'm beat." She nodded toward their car as it pulled up at the curb.

Their driver opened the car door, and he watched Lily slide inside before the door closed behind her. Ford followed the driver around and let himself in the opposite side so she wouldn't be forced to scoot across the seat in that tight pink dress. The interior was cool and quiet, welcome after the lively chatter of the crowd. With the privacy screen closed, he and Lily were ensconced in the hushed shell of the Town Car's backseat.

Being home for the short fall recess meant that they'd seen each other more in the last several weeks than in the previous months since they'd met and started dating. Ford didn't know if it was the frequent togetherness, the intimate environment of the quiet backseat, or the exhaustion after sharing in her friend's emotional day, but Lily scooted close to him and snuggled into him when he draped his arm over her bare shoulders. With her head resting on his shoulder, he only had to turn his head to press a kiss into her hair before inhaling her floral shampoo. She fit there, at his side, in his arms.

"Sunday fun day, tomorrow?" he asked, though he wasn't sure she hadn't drifted off to sleep, lulled by the gentle hum of the tires on the street.

She started at his voice, probably close to nodding off. "Not for me, I'm afraid. I've been so wrapped up with Carly's wedding that I've neglected my own stuff. Everything's starting to catch up with me." She sounded sleepy, the sexy rasp of her drowsy voice making it harder to imagine saying goodbye forever. All he could picture was hearing that voice murmuring from the pillow next to his in the darkness. He had to stop before he said or did something foolish.

"You have vital model business to attend to?" he joked, giving himself a mental shake and lightening his tone.

"Yeah, I have a crucial tanning appointment tomorrow. It just can't wait another day." She laughed. "No, actually, I have another meeting with our team about the nonprofit organization I'm trying to get off the ground on Monday. My dad offered to come over tomorrow to catch me up on everything I've missed."

"On a Sunday? You are some dedicated people."

"I want to be on the same page as everyone else, especially since they've all been so nice about the time I spent helping Carly with the wedding. Plus, we just got word on some important funding coming through, so we're eager to stay focused."

"This is the group that's going to help military widows, right?" He knew Lily had gone to college, and anyone who spent any time with her knew that she was more than just a pretty face, but he never would've expected her to be so heavily involved with starting a nonprofit. It was a refreshing surprise.

"That's the one. It's called Soldier On, and of course we're still working out exactly what's practical for us to offer. The primary purpose is to provide services for military widows and widowers who are having trouble reintegrating into civilian life."

"Wow. That's a big task to take on, but you know, I can't think off the top of my head of any group around here offering the same thing." They rarely talked about Lily's first husband, but he knew the basics. No doubt she'd gotten the idea for her organization from her personal experience. She was remarkably well-versed in the needs of military widows and seemed passionate about her cause. Why hadn't she talked about it more before tonight? Because he'd never asked? Not for the first time, he realized how much of their time together was spent doing what he wanted and talking about himself.

"Exactly. It's an underserved population, one that most people don't consider in need, probably because everyone's so vocal with their support. Support doesn't always last, though, or even translate to any kind of real assistance. Eventually, I'd love if we could function as a one-stop shop for these people leaving military life and returning to civilian status. They need resource referrals, financial assistance, employment service, education, you name it. Some of them have relied on their spouse's income and have moved around so much they never put down firm roots. They need somewhere they can turn to make the changes a little less overwhelming."

"So, what's the end game? Are you planning to run this on the side while everyone stays at their jobs, or are you looking to make a more permanent switch?"

"Honestly? I hadn't thought much about it until recently because it's always felt like such an abstract concept. Now that it's really coming together and it looks like we'll make this thing a reality, I think I'll make it my full-time job."

"Wow, so no more modeling?"

"I could see myself going out for the odd job now and then, but otherwise, yeah, no more modeling. I'm ready to make a change. More often than not, I'll be on set and all I can think about is new ideas for Soldier On or solving one of the problems that have cropped up. I've seen so much of the world and met a lot of incredible people, but this organization is what I actually care about."

"I'm sure you bring a unique perspective to the table, one that really helps focus your mission."

"Absolutely. I didn't have most of the problems we'll be addressing, but I know what the women are going through. I've known plenty of women who could've benefited from a place like this. My problems have been more with securing the initial funding as well as figuring out how we plan to keep the doors open and the lights on for the long term. I think we're talking fundraising tomorrow."

"Ah, fundraising. My favorite." Did anyone enjoy fundraising?

"Yeah, I guess you know more than most that it's a necessary evil. I'll do whatever I need to do but never imagined how difficult it would be to get funding. I guess I thought money would follow the idea." She laughed softly, gesturing in the darkened car. "I came up with this big idea but realized pretty quickly that I don't know the first thing about starting or running a nonprofit. My degree is in social work, but I've never even worked in my field. My dad is on the board, and he's got a ton of experience working in social services. It's been helpful when it comes to the nuts and bolts, and it's really just nice to have something we love to do together."

"My dad was very involved in my first campaign. We had a good experience, but I think it was a bit much for him. Working with family is one of those things that can go either way, I guess."

"Oh yeah. I wasn't sure how it would work out with us, but it's been great so far. We've tackled some big issues together, and so far, so good. Our next big hurdle will be finding a building. That might do us in." She laughed. "Unless we find an amazing real estate agent, the stress could get to us."

Ford may have grown up in the isolated luxury of wealth, surrounded by people who'd never known hardship, but he spent a considerable amount of time in his district. He wasn't ignorant to the way people lived, the way real people struggled with everyday life. Any organization that helped women and men get back on their feet after losing their spouses in service to the country was one that he'd support. Getting involved with Soldier On could be a great way to pay Lily back for all the time and attention she'd given to him.

"Do you need anything? I could help." The thought of spending time with Lily as well as doing something to help such a worthy cause was intriguing.

She sat up, and while her focused attention was amazing, he missed having her in his arms. "Would you have time?"

"That depends on what you need, but I'd be happy to do what I can."

"Aren't you super focused on your re-election? I mean, I know you're kind of getting down to the wire with the campaigning this time of year."

"I don't spend all my time campaigning. I'm here with you tonight, aren't I?"

"You know what I mean. Your work time."

"I hate to point out the obvious, but the families who benefit from your organization might vote, and fundraiser events are typically full of voters as well. But that's not why I offered." She dropped her gaze, and he continued. "Your idea has a lot of promise, and I'd like to help."

When she looked back up, he knew if he gave himself half a chance, he could get lost in those eyes. "Thank you. I hate to take advantage of you, but we could really use a big name."

"It's not taking advantage; I offered. Besides, it'll be nice to help you out for once."

"What do you mean?"

"Having you at my side helps every single time we go out. Every fundraiser, every social cocktail hour, every photo op. I invite you because I enjoy your company, but I'd be lying if I said it wasn't good for my campaign. You definitely make me look good."

She grinned, her eyes reflecting flashes of light from passing traffic. "I never thought of it like that, so you're welcome." Her light laugh wrapped around him in the car's dark interior. "Seriously, though, one thing we're lacking is publicity. It would be amazing if we could get a spot on *Good Morning, Dallas*. If you have a good contact there, I would really appreciate an introduction. Maybe I could get them to book us for an interview spot."

"I actually do know the woman who books their guests, and she is easy to work with, so that's no problem. Consider it done." Glad he could help, he enjoyed the soft weight of her settling into the crook of his arm as they rode on.

Chapter Two

Monday morning, Springsteen wailed about being born to run, and the air conditioner's cool breeze cut through the warm fall morning as Ford pulled into his campaign headquarters parking lot. His personal assistant and right hand, Joelle, parked beside his car, already pulling bags over her shoulder as she slid out of her car to meet him. Her average, motherly appearance became radiant, like she was an angel sent from heaven, when she pressed a steaming cup of coffee into his hand.

"Good morning." He sipped the scorching liquid and gave her a grateful smile. "Ah, you're a lifesaver."

"Just doing what I have to do to get to work with the human version of Ford Richardson today." She grinned, and he thought not for the first time that he'd be lost without her steadfast service. Ford couldn't wait to promote Joelle to assistant to the governor of the great state of Texas. Her talents were wasted on working for a congressman, but all things in good time. For now, they'd focus on winning his congressional re-election in November.

The unseasonably warm sunshine slowed his stride. Surely it was the weather and not the fact that his opponent was killing him in the polls that dampened his mood. Joelle delivered updates and handed him the corresponding papers as they walked, or scurried as was the case with her. He had a good foot and a half on her and took one step for every two of hers. He juggled the folders and coffee in one hand to hold the door open for her when they reached the building. Staffers and volunteers were already at work, making phone calls, meeting to plan strategies, analyzing data, and proofreading campaign materials. It was a buzzing hive of activity, and there was no place on earth he loved more, whether he was winning or losing. He cut through the crowd, offering his "good mornings" as he made a straight shot for his office at the other end of the room.

He sipped his coffee, perking up as the rich elixir worked its way into his sleepy system. "What's first on the agenda?" he asked as he settled into his chair and Joelle seated herself across from him. She crossed her legs and balanced her planner on her knee, scanning the entries. The voicemail light on his office phone was blinking, but he focused his attention on his assistant.

"Strategy meeting in—" She glanced at the clock. "Five minutes. Sorry. I should have told you to come in earlier." She winced, clearly not convinced that he could switch gears so quickly. He hadn't won his first term in office by being slow to adapt. Prepping for an early morning meeting with no time to spare was a cakewalk in comparison.

"It's no problem; I'm ready for it. Anything urgent that you want to get off your plate before I go in?" He glanced out into the office. The glass walls and door sometimes reminded him of being an animal in a zoo exhibit, but it was temporary, and he wanted to be fully present. It was good for him to be able to see everything, and he knew that staffers felt more connected when he wasn't hidden away in some office.

"Your mother would like you to meet her for lunch at the club sometime this week. She said she couldn't get a hold of you herself." Joelle's smirk said that he owed her one for running interference. "And so she called me. Repeatedly. In addition to leaving multiple voicemails."

Joelle deserved a raise for fielding those calls. His mother was nothing if not persistent. "Sorry about that. How does she manage to get along without me when I'm in D.C.? I'll be there, and I'll call her to confirm myself. You're off the hook, and thank you for handling that." When Jessica Woodall Richardson invited you to lunch, it wasn't exactly a request. "What else is going on this afternoon?"

She scanned his schedule, ran a highlighter over a couple of entries, and handed him the page. "I left you a bit of a cushion so you'd have a little wiggle room if lunch runs long, so after that, you just have the Senior Citizen Center dedication this afternoon."

"Don't want to miss that." Besides being one of his pet projects, the place was full of Republicans who voted early and often.

On his way to the conference room for the weekly strategy meeting, he took a moment to appreciate the room full of people, all there working on his behalf. His father, the venerable judge Rutherford Buchanan Richardson, Jr., had taught him that. Voters elected people, not ideas, and personal relationships were paramount. He never forgot that, never discounted it. Every facet of his campaign, from the smallest details of the headquarters office layout, to the way he interacted with everyone on his staff, reflected that importance.

"Good morning, everyone," he greeted the assembled dream team as he took his seat at the conference table.

The serious faces lining the table were unreadable, though he knew each of the seven people better than almost anyone. He'd been with the same team since the inception of his first congressional run. Of all the people buzzing around his campaign, these five men and two women were the only ones likely to give him the straight truth, no false hope or shielding him from negatives. He needed it, welcomed it, but today, the heavy atmosphere in the room made him wonder if he might want to avoid it.

"What's the latest?" He began the meeting with optimism, though little of it was reflected in the faces surrounding him.

Charlie Tibbals, the most senior member of the team, cleared his throat. Charlie had worked for Ford's father, and there was no one in the world he trusted more with his career. "It's Coldwell. He's gaining on you in the polls, and we haven't been able to do much about it."

Was it getting worse? His first campaign had been relatively easy, at least as far as congressional races went, and he wasn't prepared for the constant battle he'd faced ever since Sam Coldwell showed up to oppose his run for re-election. If he only had to face the Democratic candidate, things would've been so much easier. Republicans don't have much difficulty winning in Texas. The rise of the Tea Party and their prevalence in the state was a challenge the team hadn't anticipated.

"Ugh. What is it now?" It was always *something*. His opponent was relentless, as opponents often were, but also possibly the most irritating human on the planet. Sam Coldwell was new money, ultra-conservative, and of course saw himself as the perfect candidate to replace Congressman Richardson, who Coldwell insisted couldn't understand his constituents. Coldwell loved pointing out their lifestyle and background differences, as though that had real bearing on how Ford executed his duties.

Charlie answered. "He's pushing his family values platform like crazy, playing up his perfect conservative persona. His supporters are eating it up." Coldwell's entire campaign had been focused on courting the churches and family groups to the exclusion of discussing any real issues, trotting out his perfect wife and son. "Oh, and in case you didn't hear, Mrs. Coldwell is pregnant with their second child. If I didn't know better, I'd say it was specifically timed to help his campaign. He's pandering to the bubbleheads who allow themselves to be distracted enough to think that the fact that you don't have a wife and kids means that you have no idea how regular people live. He's managed to present himself as the ultimate candidate for constituents who love the lord, their wives, and their kids, and worse, that you're the polar opposite." Charlie took a sip of his coffee and shook his head.

"Remember the good old days when we only had to worry about Democrats? These Tea Party candidates are relentless; it's always about who's more conservative." Ford rubbed his forehead in irritation. "It's as though the issues don't matter, as long as you're more conservative than the other guy."

"He must have some amazing speech writers, because as absurd as the whole thing is, he's convincing voters. People are starting to buy into the idea that you're not a good conservative because you're not married. This is a problem."

Ford sat back in his chair and held his palms up. "Well, what can I do? I can't just turn into some family man overnight. If I could materialize the perfect nuclear family, I'd consider it. Too bad I can't." Not having a wife or kids at thirty-two didn't mean Ford didn't understand the issues facing families in his constituency, but that didn't stop voters from believing it.

Charlie straightened a stack of file folders and pushed them toward Ford. "Maybe you can't, but this is a start."

He flipped open the top folder, finding a woman's photograph and information sheets clamped to either side. "What is this?"

"After careful analysis of Coldwell's campaign and voter response, we've determined the best course of action is for you to find a wife." Charlie wasn't laughing, but surely this was a joke.

Ford put his coffee down instead of taking a sip. The woman in the folder was lovely and didn't deserve to have a hot beverage spewed on her face. "Come again?"

"I know it seems extreme, but believe me, you wouldn't be the first candidate to use an engagement to his advantage. Since time is of the essence, we've done the legwork and found some possible matches for you. These are some solid choices." He tapped the stack of folders. "You can read through their bios to familiarize yourself with their basic information, and then we will set up a series of meetings so you can get to know some or all of them. These women have been thoroughly vetted, and they have spotless backgrounds and airtight confidentiality agreements."

"Forgive me, but are you serious?" Why was he the only one at the table who understood how absurd the discussion was?

"I know it's not ideal, but face it, you're not exactly a hopeless romantic." His oldest friend and trusted team member, Robert, chimed in. "The chances of you meeting some incredible woman right now, falling in love, and getting engaged within our optimal timeframe are microscopic. This makes it easy, and you could do a lot worse than choosing one of these women."

Ford had been a romantic once, but that was a long time ago. "I hear what you're saying; I really do. But still, I don't think I should be choosing women out of a stack of folders. I might as well be going to the pound to adopt a puppy."

The team laughed, but Ford didn't see the humor. Charlie spoke up first. "Try not to think of it as a love match. It's more like choosing someone to be a piece in the campaign puzzle. You have partners for every other aspect of your campaign, and this isn't much different. The best way to get the focus off of your personal life and onto the issues and your voting record is to give the appearance of having a personal life. A wife accomplishes that handily." Probably seeing that Ford wasn't convinced, Charlie paused before conceding. "You can limit your commitment to an engagement if you're uncomfortable with the idea of going through with an actual legal marriage under these conditions. We certainly don't want you to compromise your personal beliefs, but you're getting killed in the polls because you're not seen as a man who values marriage and family."

"I'm already seeing someone. It's not incredibly serious, but I don't think she'd like it if I got engaged to someone else out of nowhere." He drummed his fingers on the stack of folders and wondered if Lily would even mind if he stopped seeing her. He'd enjoyed their casual relationship, but perhaps they were a little too casual.

Robert snapped his fingers. "Oh yeah, that model? How about her?"

"Like I said," Ford began slowly as though he were speaking to a child. "Things between us aren't serious. I don't think she'd be comfortable getting engaged just yet." Or ever, not that he even knew what she wanted. She'd been married before, but her first husband had been killed in combat mere months after their wedding. She didn't seem eager to move on and was clearly happy staying single.

As was he.

"Perhaps it's time to have a conversation with her about taking the next logical step in your relationship. Either that, or consider the candidates we've found for you." Caroline sat back in her chair, folding her arms as though the matter were settled.

He and Lily had never once brought up the subject of marriage, and he couldn't predict what her reaction would be if he did. "So, what next? I give them the wife, and then they wonder why I don't have children? Do you have a stack of folders with adorable kids for me to choose from? What about the perfect family dog while we're at it? Do you have a selection of ranch style homes in great suburban neighborhoods? Where does it stop?" The idea was absurd, and Ford knew his reaction was snowballing out of control, but surely they had to see that this wouldn't work.

"We'll just take it one step at a time," Charlie said calmly, as though Ford were overreacting. "There's no need to panic."

"I'm not panicking," he said, though fleeing the room seemed like a good idea. "I'm simply pointing out the fact that this is absurd. I can't believe we're even discussing this."

"Do us a favor, and at least consider it. You can either ask your current girlfriend or take a look through the candidates' files. If one of them seems like someone you could work with, we'll call her in for a meeting. No need to get ahead of ourselves, and definitely no need to freak out over this." Robert's tone said that Ford was a man who needed to be talked down off the ledge, though he was clearly the only sane person left in the room.

"You guys can all stop looking at me like I'm the crazy one. You're sitting there asking me, no telling me, to either propose to someone I've been casually dating or to pick a wife out of a stack of what? Half a dozen folders? This is outrageous." Ford sat back in his chair, not sure if he should laugh or leave.

Charlie was unmoved by his outburst. "Listen, it's our job to figure out where your campaign is weak, and that's what we've done. Your opponent is running all over town convincing people that you're not a good candidate because of your marital status. That's something we can fix very easily."

"And I suppose reasoning with voters isn't a possibility? There's no chance we can address the rhetoric and remind them that I'm an individual and not having a wife doesn't make me an inferior legislator?" Ford knew without a doubt he was being reasonable. Why nobody else around the table could see that was beyond him.

"You know as well as anyone that acknowledging when your opponents point out your weakness can make you seem defensive, and I'm sure you'll also agree that there's not enough time to turn popular opinion around on this issue before Election Day. It seems like you have two choices. Either find a fiancée, or spend all your time addressing the reasons you don't have one, at the expense of the issues you actually care about." Charlie sat forward, leaning on his elbows, and looked Ford in the eye. This was no joke.

He flipped through the folders, a dull ache forming behind his right eye. Each woman was beautiful and clearly chosen with respect to her "candidate's wife" appearance. They were all degreed professionals with clean criminal background checks who would be willing to stay at home with their children or quit their jobs if his campaign needs required it. Ugh. Who would be willing to give up her career for a man she hadn't met? He respected the hell out of stay-at-home mothers. He'd been raised by one, and nobody in their right mind would argue that she was less competent or influential because she didn't have a job. The idea of a woman being so committed to her marriage and family was appealing, but he'd never ask someone to derail her professional aspirations for him—though it would be amazing to be worth that much to someone. Hell, the mere suggestion that there was a woman alive who would care so much about him was enough to set his mind racing, but this wasn't genuine. A woman being so eager to marry a congressman, anyone, that she'd be willing to agree to it before so much as meeting him turned his stomach. That wasn't love. That was desperation and social climbing, and he definitely wouldn't be bringing children into any such transaction. He wondered if Lily had ever thought about having children

"We don't see any way around this, not if you want to win the election." Charlie checked his watch, the fluorescent overhead lights glinting off the face. "Think it over if you need time. I'll set up some meetings when you've decided who you'd like to meet. Or I'll get started on your concession speech. Your choice."

•••

Across town at a photo shoot, Lily mentally transported herself to a sunny Hawaiian beach, squishing warm sand between her toes while a hibiscus-scented breeze gently ruffled her hair. If she concentrated, she could smell the coconut sunscreen on her skin and the cool weight of the fruity daiquiri in her hand. Anything to get her mind off the pain in her arm, burning and screaming at her to stretch, to move, to do anything but continue to hold perfectly still.

"Beautiful, that's wonderful," the photographer murmured as he snapped away. "If you could turn your wrist just a little to the right, please." He waited while she adjusted. "That's it, thank you, love."

Click, click, click. Shots from every angle.

The bright lights burned her eyes, and before long, the sweat beads forming at her hairline would snake down her face, ruining her makeup if she didn't do something. Surely the photographer would get the shot before her limbs gave up on her. They were shooting a luxury handbag ad, but the gorgeous bag dangling precariously from her manicured fingertips was little more than an afterthought in the exotic layout. Lily was almost glad they'd dressed her in nothing more than a lacy bra and panties set, since the set lights were so hot her thick, stylized makeup was about to melt off her face. She was perched on a fuchsia velvet chaise, her legs positioned so that she was supported on the very edge, but just barely, holding a squirmy snow-white Persian kitten in the hand not burdened with the handbag. The prospect of returning her legs to a natural angle and taking a long, refreshing drink of ice cold water was enough to tide her over. If her years of professional modeling had taught her anything, it was that getting the shot right the first time, no matter how uncomfortable she was, was always preferable to getting stuck going for round after round until it was right.

The buttery-soft, petal pink leather of the handbag she was holding was what she imagined angel feathers felt like. Good lord, it was a gorgeous bag. She'd been lucky to book such a good campaign. Prestige retailer, local shoot, wide distribution. At twenty-seven, she couldn't ask for much more, and yet, there was so much more that she wanted.

"I think we've got it, doll. Thank you." The photographer lowered his camera and motioned to his assistant to take his equipment.

With a mind of their own, her arms immediately fell to her sides once a perky blonde photographer's assistant collected the kitten resting in her lap. Another assistant retrieved the handbag, plucking it unceremoniously from her hands. Finally free to flex and stretch, her fingers sang out in relief as she moved, slowly returning to her human form. Pulling herself up from the set, she debated heading over to craft services for the ice cold water she'd dreamed about before even slipping into the robe hanging just off set waiting for her. The whole crew had been watching her pose in a lacy bra and panty set all day anyway, so what was a little bit longer?

To her great relief, she didn't have to choose. A young, blond man dressed in black skinny jeans and a skintight black tee shirt pushed a cold water bottle into her hand. "Thank you." Her gravelly voice sounded like she'd found an oasis in the desert, and it wasn't far from the truth. Slipping one arm into the robe while the other held the bottle to her lips, she quenched her thirst and protected what was left of her modesty.

Her eyes fell on a wall-mounted clock, and she choked on her sip. The shoot had run much longer than she anticipated, and if she didn't get back into street clothes and halfway across town in the next thirty minutes, she'd be late. The only chance she had at creating a more fulfilling career for herself, for actually using her social work degree for something more than a coaster, was to make it happen. Her father and a small board of directors were likely already well on their way to the planning meeting of the nonprofit organization she was starting.

After her husband, Nathan, died, she realized how close she'd come to becoming one of the women she knew who lost their husbands and had nowhere to turn when it was time to rebuild their lives. She'd been exposed to army life so briefly, but many of the women and men married to soldiers that Nathan knew had been entrenched in military culture. Never in her wildest dreams would she have imagined that she'd be looking at Soldier On becoming a reality. She should have, though, because her parents were enthusiastic social activists, and her dad was always ready to jump on a great idea. He had gone straight to work, using his community connections and experience from years of working in social services. It was perfect, really, since he knew nonprofits from the inside out.

Coming in late and in absurdly heavy makeup was not exactly the best way to inspire confidence. She could either be on time, or she could be bare-faced. Not both. Soldier On was her dream, and she didn't want to waste time getting ready. The board would get a laugh when she showed up with the elaborate makeup, but she'd be there on time.

Ducking out of the crowd of crew members and company executives, she rushed to the dressing room for the quickest wardrobe change of her life. After shoving her legs into jeans and yanking a light sweater over her head, she pushed her feet into a pair of ballet flats and practically ran out the door. The afternoon traffic was already building, and the sun was squarely in her eyes for the entire drive to the downtown conference room they'd rented, but she made it.

Her dad sat at the head of the table, barely suppressing a smile at her appearance when Lily finally blew into the meeting, out of breath and sweating like she was still under the hot lights. "Glad you could join us," he teased.

Lily took her seat at the table and pulled a bottle of water out of her bag. As she listened to a recap of their last meeting, she unscrewed the top and focused on slowing her breath. Her phone vibrated, showing a line of missed texts from Ford. He must have forgotten that she was working all day and then meeting with the board members. Typical. She enjoyed the casual dating relationship she shared with the congressman, but he didn't seem to take her schedule quite as seriously as he did his own. He probably needed her to attend a fundraiser or some kind of facility opening for a photo opportunity.

The group continued with the meeting as she pushed her phone to the side and focused on the folder full of information she'd been handed. "Is this current?" The timeline on her information sheet showed that they could be operational a full six months earlier than she'd anticipated.

Her father gave her a wide smile. "It's all there. We have some serious needs that must be met before we'll truly be up and running on all cylinders, but if all goes according to plan, this project is all systems go. We got word on the grant late last week, so we know the basics will be covered. That's all we need to push forward."

Her phone buzzed again, skipping gently on the table.

Ford. Again.

For a casual relationship, he certainly was persistent.

She sneaked a peek this time, wondering vaguely if he could have an actual urgent need.

She could forgive the excessive texting, in gratitude for him being willing to be her date for Carly's wedding. She'd been nervous about inviting him to be her plus one, knowing how many men read too much into being asked to go to a wedding, but he'd been wonderful. Attending with Ford meant she had been able to enjoy the events without having to worry about keeping a date at arm's length, always watching what she said so he wouldn't get the wrong idea. He knew the score, and he was on board. They always had a good time together, but that was it. No spending the night, no talk of the future, no wondering if this relationship was going anywhere. Because it wasn't. Ford was fun to be around, interesting and smart, and incredibly charming. They had undeniable chemistry, but every time she was tempted to give in to her attraction to him or her desire to take things further emotionally, she'd think of Nathan. She and Ford saw each other every time he was in town, but he was in D.C. much of the year, giving her the opportunity to carefully tamp down any developing feelings before she let things go too far. If he wondered why she never responded to his unspoken advances, to those times when their kisses were heading in the direction of becoming more, he was too much of a gentleman to push her and mention it.

The meeting wrapped up, and she read his most recent text.

Ford: *I know you have a meeting after work, but would you text or call when you have a minute?*

Smiling to herself, she tapped out her reply: *Hey, what's up?*

Ford: *Are you free tonight? I need to talk with you.*

Lily: *Um, sure. Is everything okay?*

Ford: *Everything's fine. I'll come over if that's okay. Say around 7?*

Lily: *Sounds good. See you then.*

Chapter Three

That afternoon, Ford followed the hostess to his mother's table in the Golden Eagle country club dining room. Jessica Woodall Richardson's posture was ramrod straight as she watched the golfers on the ninth hole outside the window. To the casual observer, she probably appeared to be lost in thought, a woman doing nothing more than enjoying a leisurely afternoon. Ford knew better. She'd likely known he'd arrived from the moment his tires hit the parking lot. That may be a bit of an exaggeration, but the fabled mother's eyes in the back of her head had only sharpened over the years. He leaned over, kissed her cheek in greeting, inhaling her signature Chanel No. 5, and indulged her when she appeared surprised that he'd arrived.

"Oh, Rutherford, dear. I'm so glad you could make it." She tucked a strand of her silver bob behind an ear, revealing a huge diamond stud earring. Rivulets of condensation snaked down the side of her water goblet, and he wondered whether she'd already ordered her midday chardonnay, or if she'd waited for him.

"Me too, Mother." He held his tie against his shirt as he sat across from her. Lunch at the club was buffet style, but he knew better than to fill his plate before she decided it was time to eat.

A waiter arrived bearing a glass of white wine, and she accepted it with a regal nod. After a delicate sip, she dabbed her lips with the linen napkin and rose. "Let's get some lunch. I'm starving."

Back at the table, Ford dug into his risotto, salmon with pesto, and asparagus spears while Mother picked at a few dry assorted greens and a tiny piece of salmon. She sipped her wine and leveled him with a disappointed look, though even a thorough search of his memory revealed no slights or wrongdoing. What had he done this time?

"I'm glad you could spare an afternoon for me before you go back to D.C." Ah, there it was.

"I'll be here for the rest of the month, except for a few days here and there, and of course I always have time to see you. I'll be in town for in-district work and campaigning until we reconvene after the election. If I do, in fact, still have a seat to return to and I'm not cleaning out my desk." He was a dutiful son, kept in touch consistently, attended family functions, and showed up for family dinners. His mother was never happier than when she was Queen Martyr, though, dishing out guilt like it was birthday cake.

"I hope you weren't hoping for a leisurely fall recess." She fanned herself dramatically. "I don't know how anybody gets anything done this time of year, between the holidays and the elections. Speaking of, how's the campaign going?"

"Fine, I guess." He speared a bite of fish, not sure it was wise to broach the subject of his possible engagement. The team was right; the quickest way to shoot down Coldwell's criticism of his single status was to get engaged. If he had to choose from the list of strangers, he likely would've dismissed the idea outright. But having Lily as an option made the idea a bit less outrageous.

"Hmm. That doesn't sound fine to me. What's the matter, sweetheart?" She set down her fork and folded her hands in her lap, concentrating on his face. She wasn't a warm, touchy-feely mother, but she did fully support his congressional campaign.

"Sam Coldwell." He took a long drink of ice water, figuring *what the hell, can't hurt to tell her*. "He's killing me on the family values front. It's gotten bad enough that we have to do something, and fast."

"Who is this Coldwell, anyway? I'd never even heard of any Coldwells before this one decided to go after your seat. Besides, I can't imagine that anyone listens to him. If anyone is firmly rooted in family, it's you." She drained her glass and pushed it to the edge of the table.

"He's attacking me on the fact that I'm not married with children like he is." He clenched his fist. "And according to my advisors, it's working."

"Oh, I see." She had the grace to avoid his gaze. The fact that he wasn't married was a sore subject between them.

"Yeah." He set his lips in a grim line, both sorry he'd brought it up and perversely glad to put it out in the open again. Nothing ruffled Jessica Richardson. Nothing except being reminded of how her merciless meddling had ended his first and only serious relationship.

"That's unfortunate. Well, I can't apologize any more than I already have." She sat up straighter, summoning her signature poise. Not for the first time, he wondered if an actual steel rod supported her spine.

"I don't want another apology. It's ancient history, and we can't turn back the clock now, can we? I need to figure out what I'm going to do about my marital status."

"What do you mean? What do they want you to do about it? If you're not married, you're not married." Her eyes were wide, and she leaned forward.

"Charlie says the only way to win this thing is to get engaged." He pushed risotto around his plate, his appetite gone.

"Really? That doesn't sound like Charlie." She raised her eyebrows, but her forehead remained unlined. Jessica Richardson was on a first name basis with her plastic surgeon and was practically married to her aesthetician.

"Oh, he is definitely on board, but I think it's insane." He kept his tone even, but he could almost see the wheels turning in Mother's mind, and he wouldn't encourage her.

"I don't know about that, dear. It's past time you found someone and settled down. And if it helps your campaign, then why not now? Mimi Fields's daughter is single." She snapped her perfectly-manicured fingers. "And so is Leila Mitchell's daughter.

I could invite them for drinks if you want. We need to get ahead on planning our winter program for Ladies' Auxiliary anyway." She reveled in her role as queen bee at home, the only female in a family full of testosterone, and saw no reason why her reach shouldn't extend to her social circles. She'd ruled over her husband and three sons with great relish when the children were still at home, and now that they had all moved out, she looked for opportunities to exert her influence.

She looked positively gleeful at the prospect of playing matchmaker, which made him want to revisit the file folders of pre-screened candidates. The only thing worse than Mother ruining his first chance at marriage would be to have her arranging the second.

"Thank you, but that won't be necessary. I'm seeing someone already, and if it doesn't work out with her, the team assembled a group of candidates for me to choose from. The whole thing is ridiculous, though, and I'm not sure if I'm going through with it or not, so don't get any ideas."

"Rutherford, it's not ridiculous. This is real life, and what voters think matters, whether you think it's a valid concern or not. If this is the only thing holding you back from a win, I don't understand refusing to address it. Why let a silly little technicality ruin your chances at re-election?" Nobody else used his full name, and she reserved her right to do so whenever she pleased.

"I don't think it's a silly little technicality, Mother. We're talking about a real, legal marriage to an actual human being—someone with feelings and a family, someone who could get hurt. That's not something I want to consider part of my re-election strategy."

"Well, when you say it like that, it sounds bad. Thinking of it that way will get you nowhere. You hire staff for every other aspect of the campaign, and this doesn't have to be any different. Consider it a strategic partnership, and it won't seem so strange. You'll hardly be the first candidate to do something like this."

She took a miniscule bite of her salmon. "You can probably wait until after the election to decide if you want to proceed with the marriage. See? One step at a time, no muss, no fuss." She sipped from her water glass. "What's wrong with giving the people what they want if it will help move things along?"

"I have my limits. Besides, I doubt Lily would appreciate me getting engaged to some random person if she doesn't happen to be ready to take things to the next level just yet." He didn't want to bring Lily into the conversation, not with his mother, but she was starting to warm to the engagement idea a bit too much. Time to shut it down.

"Why haven't we met this mystery woman?" She narrowed her eyes, the same piercing blue that he saw in the mirror staring back at him. After her merciless interference in his past romantic relationships, her suspicion was hilarious. She knew exactly why he wouldn't bring up a relationship with her.

"Because it's a new relationship, and we're not serious yet." And the whole thing was none of her business, but he wouldn't say that to her face.

"Well, what about her, then? Just take the natural next step and propose to her. Talk about an easy solution." She waved her hand as though the problem was solved.

If he'd been drinking at the moment, he would've spit water on Mother's perfectly pressed cream St. John suit. He could just imagine how Lily would react to a proposal after their months of deliberately casual dating. "I don't think so. Like I said, it's not serious."

"Well, who is she anyway?" To Mother, no woman in her right mind would turn up her nose at the chance to marry a congressman, a Richardson of the old-money, high society Dallas Richardsons no less. A Richardson might as well be a Rockefeller, for goodness sake.

"Her name is Lily Ashton. She's a model."

Mother wrinkled her nose and then quickly hid her distaste with a saccharin smile. "She must be the young lady I've seen you with in the paper. And what a lovely name, Lily. I'd like to meet her."

"Here's something you may be interested in. You know the wedding I went to on Saturday?"

"Yes, of course. The reason you couldn't meet us for dinner with the Carlisles."

"The bride was Lily's best friend, Carly Piper from that *Around the World in Thirteen Cakes* show you pretend you only watch because the housekeeper DVRs it."

Her eyes lit up with interest. Mother had an unhealthy obsession with The Cuisine Network, an interesting choice for someone who rarely ate anything substantial.

"Carly Piper? I adore her and that handsome man who does the show with her. I saw their engagement episode when they were in Paris. Very romantic."

"Maybe I can get an autograph for you."

"Don't be silly." She snapped her fingers. "You should see if they still make wedding cakes when you get engaged. Their work is phenomenal."

Years of practice made it possible for him to refrain from rolling his eyes. "Okay, Mother, I'll do just that."

Ford checked his watch. "I need to run." He leaned over and kissed her temple before leaving. "Nice to see you."

"You too, dear." She was already waving to a friend across the dining room when he reached the door.

Chapter Four

Later that evening, Ford sank into the plush cushions of Lily's sofa and sipped his wine as he lazily pushed the little golden elephant he'd given her across the end table, looking right at home. After working and sitting in the planning meeting for her new non-profit organization all day, she was ready for a break, and he was definitely easy on the eyes. They'd made a lot of progress at the board meeting, and she was finally catching up, but wondering what was going on with Ford made it hard to relax and catch her breath. When he'd asked to meet her, it sounded urgent. Now that he was here, it could've been any other evening. Either he wasn't as concerned about whatever it was as he'd let on, or he was much cooler under pressure than she'd realized. He was taking his time, checking out her apartment and sipping his wine. He'd given her the wine a month ago, a gorgeous pinot noir, and no matter how many times it happened, Lily wondered if she'd ever be comfortable accepting gifts from him. There was a lot she still didn't know about Rutherford Buchanan Richardson, III—like what kind of family would hoist that name upon a little boy, continuing the family legacy or not.

She set her own glass on the coffee table and joined him on the sofa. When he met her eye, she saw the tension she'd sensed earlier. Ford didn't usually stay inside her apartment for long when they went out. Always the gentleman, he'd come up to collect her, but he'd never spent any significant amount of time in her home. She wasn't sure if he was trying to keep things casual, or if he was uncomfortable being in her apartment under the watchful eyes of her late husband's photographs and memories. Her space wasn't one big shrine to Nathan, but there was definitely evidence of him.

Had there been bad news for his campaign? Or was it something else? Was he breaking up with her? Could you break up with someone who wasn't officially your girlfriend? What was going on?

She glanced at the clock and stopped the runaway train of questions in her mind. If he was going to end their relationship or whatever it was, he needed to do it and get out so she could catch up on the backlog of shows waiting on her DVR. *Downton Abbey* wasn't going to watch itself. Surprisingly, the thought of never seeing him again squeezed her heart a little. She'd miss him, miss what they had together, which was nothing, really, so she'd be fine. She'd just have to remind herself of that.

"So, there was something you wanted to talk to me about?" She sounded lame even to her own ears, but the suspense was killing her.

"Yes, and thank you for having me over. I thought it would be nice to have some privacy." Ford shifted on the sofa and took a long sip of his wine. "This is really good, by the way." He swirled the ruby liquid, keeping his eyes on the hand-blown glass she'd bought on a trip to Spain.

"It should be. You gave it to me."

"Oh?" He laughed, a bit nervously. "I guess I have great taste in wine." He put his glass down and ran his hands across his thighs, looking nervous. "I'll definitely have to bring this one next time, too."

"That sounds great." She pulled her feet under her, still uneasy but not quite so worried he was about to bolt now that they'd made vague plans for the future. The bigger question was why she cared one way or the other, but she'd tuck that away for later.

"Did you get caught up on everything today? I know you had that important meeting with your board."

As pleased as she was that he'd remembered and asked, he wasn't there to find out about how her emerging enterprise was coming along. "We did. Sure, it was an intense day, but we needed to buckle down and get things ironed out. I won't let myself get that far behind again. Fortunately, for all of us, my dad is the most passionate person on the team, and he didn't let the whole thing fall apart while I was busy with Carly's wedding."

"That's great. Can't wait to see how things come together." He cleared his throat and let his eyes wander around her apartment. Either he was interested in the décor, which was admittedly awesome, or Ford Richardson was nervous. "Listen, I have to talk to you about something, and it's a bit awkward." Finally. She wanted to shout at him to get on with it, but he looked like he might be sick.

She reached out and covered his hand with hers, surprised to find that it was trembling. "What is it? Is everything okay?"

He cleared his throat and angled his body to face her. She'd never seen him look so intense, not even during his impassioned stump speeches. Maybe he was seriously ill and didn't know how to tell her. She picked her wine glass up and took a sip, willing the smooth liquid to calm her nerves.

"I'm just going to lay it all out, just blurt it out, and then we'll figure out where to go from there." Once he got started, he didn't seem quite so afraid to continue. The shaking stopped, and he squeezed her hand. "I need a wife, and I'd like it to be you."

Her wine threatened to come out her nose, but she managed to swallow before she set the glass down. "I'm sorry, but what? I think I misheard you."

"I know, it sounds crazy, and I'm sorry for springing it on you like that."

"Um, is this a joke, or are you horrible at proposing?" Her heart raced, but why? She wasn't interested in marriage, was she? Not again, and not to Congressman Richardson, at least. Lily never even voted Republican, for Pete's sake. Strange, then, that the idea was kind of appealing.

He laughed, that rich, easy laugh that could turn her knees to jelly. "I've never proposed before. Are you saying that's not how to do it?" His smile was charming; his eyes twinkled in the low light of her living room.

Oddly enough, she wasn't compelled to shimmy down the fire escape to the street below to avoid the explanation of this strange proposal. "No, I don't think that's how you do it."

The awkward tension fizzled out of the air between them with the light joke, but Ford's eyes turned serious. "It sounds crazy, but I need a wife. Or at least a fiancée to present to the public. I don't stand a chance of re-election without it, thanks to my opponent's pandering to the lowest common denominator."

"Okay, want to explain that to the layperson?"

"My opponent, Sam Coldwell, is pushing the family values angle so hard that voters are losing sight of the real issues facing our district and the country. I run on a conservative platform, and for better or worse, I'm seen as less of a viable Republican candidate since I'm single. My opponent, on the other hand, is happily married with an adorable child and one on the way, and he never hesitates to bring them to the voters' attention. With everything else being equal, I can't beat him on the family values front since I'm not married, and that could be the one thing that loses the election for me. So..." He spread his hands, as though helpless to change the situation.

"So, what exactly are you saying?"

"My advisory team provided a list of pre-screened women who were willing to enter a political marriage, and they want me to go through the group and choose one to be my wife." He cringed. "It's even worse saying it out loud. I know how horrible that sounds, believe me."

"Yeah, I'm not sure you do." She shifted on the sofa, mind reeling from the idea of a political marriage. Her first marriage had been a dream come true, and it ended too soon. Though she'd never admitted to herself that the day would come that she would move on, some part of her knew she could, eventually. She always assumed it would be for love, though, nothing like this. Entertaining the idea of marriage wasn't something she took lightly.

"As much as I tried to convince them otherwise, the team is adamant that this is the only way. I don't know that I would actually be able to follow through and marry one of those women. I'm not a robot. But I do need a public fiancée, at least until Election Day."

"And then what?"

"Then we see what happens. If I win, there'll have to be a serious discussion on how to move forward. If I lose, then you'll be free to move on if you like. We don't have to keep it up if you'd rather not."

"Me?"

"I really hope so, Lily. I know I'm asking a lot of you, that we're nowhere near ready for marriage, but I need help. I need you. I don't want to pick a woman from the list."

"What exactly would I be agreeing to?" She couldn't believe that the conversation hadn't ended with her showing him the door already, but something made her want to hear the rest. Maybe she wasn't quite ready for marriage yet, but she wasn't ready to say goodbye to Ford. And a not-quite-real engagement was perfect for someone who wasn't ready for a real marriage. She'd never considered the possibility that any man could replace her first husband, not in her heart, and not in her life. Ford wasn't asking to take that place, though, and he knew it wasn't going to be real. This might be the ideal solution.

He smiled, clearly relieved that he hadn't been turned down without another word. "First, thank you for hearing me out. The only thing worse than having to come to you with this crazy scheme would be for you to laugh me out of your home. I could hardly get through the conversation with my team, and I've been dreading having to ask you." He sipped his wine and sat forward a bit as he explained. "We'll need a public proposal. We can discuss that later, if you agree, but it's got to be somewhere we'll have an audience and photographers. After the proposal, we'll make a formal announcement, so you'll want to tell your friends and family rather than let them be surprised when they read about it online. This engagement can't be a secret, and nobody can know that it's for the campaign. I know that probably goes without saying, but if word gets out that you are simply playing the part, then I'd be ruined." His blue eyes pleaded with her to acknowledge the gravity of the situation. "After that, you'll just have to play the part of loving fiancée. I'll need you to attend campaign stops with me, fundraisers, things like that. Pretty much the same events you've been coming to, but more of them, and with you taking a more active role. Also, you'd be more visible in the public eye, so if you're, uh, seeing anyone else, I'd have ask you to end things." They'd never even discussed whether or not their relationship was exclusive. This was crazy, but the idea was growing on her.

"I'm not seeing anyone else, but my friends and family will think I'm a nutcase. I mean, people know that I've been dating you, but nobody thinks it's serious." It wasn't serious, and it wasn't going to be. Did he think they could simply pretend otherwise in front of other people and go back to normal behind closed doors?

"We haven't been incredibly open about the nature of our relationship, so I don't think it's inconceivable that things could be more serious behind the scenes than they seem, you know. The public will buy it without a thought, and your friends and family will probably go along with it if we show them that we're a good match. I can visit with anyone who has concerns to show them that I'm a good guy, but you won't be able to tell anyone that this is an arrangement. Not even Carly or your parents. Nobody. For all intents and purposes, this will be a real engagement as far as anyone knows. We'll have a confidentiality agreement drawn up that I'll need you to sign, but we'll have a solid, believable story to tell people, so maybe it won't be as bad as you think."

"Maybe." Her parents would probably be happy to hear that she'd moved on, but her friends would likely think that she'd lost her damn mind. Pretending to suddenly be in love with Ford could prove to be exhausting, but it might be worth it. Friends were always trying to set her up with guys. At least that would stop.

"If it makes it any easier, remember that I'll be in D.C. when Congress is in session, and you're welcome to stay here if you want a break from me and the campaign circus. We could easily say that work keeps you here. I'd love to have you come with me, too, though. I have a nice apartment close to the Hill, and I'm rarely there, so you could get some breathing space. We can see how it goes, and you might decide that you want some time away and alone." And when she was home alone, she would truly be alone. There wouldn't be any phone calls, video chats, sad emails. She could be completely, blissfully, alone. This could work.

"So, if you don't win the election, we just say goodbye?"

"Not unless that's what you really want. I've really enjoyed dating you, so I don't think I'll want to end things just because we don't have to carry on with the engagement. I won't hold you to it, though. We don't have to get married, if that's what's worrying you."

"But if you do win, that's the next step, right?" She wrung her hands in her lap, wondering if she was excited or frightened by the prospect. Probably a bit of both.

He cut his eyes away from her, suddenly finding the Murano glass sculpture she'd bought in Italy very interesting. "That's the only logical conclusion, but I would never ask you to compromise your personal values. If it comes down to it and you aren't sure you can or want to marry me, we can certainly figure something out. Don't feel pressured to decide about marriage until you're ready. We can focus on the engagement, which is what I really need right now."

This was really happening. Her not-quite boyfriend was not-quite proposing, and she had a decision to make. Even without the confidentiality agreement, she couldn't hash it out with Carly, not while her friend was in Paris on her honeymoon. Besides, even considering the staged engagement was too strange to actually admit to anyone. "So, if I say no, you and I will break up, and you'll have to pick someone from your binder full of women?" Joking about it made it a little easier to handle.

That earned her a smile. "Yes, unfortunately. I can't add a cheating scandal onto my fake engagement, so you and I won't be able to see each other anymore."

That shouldn't bother her, but it did. She didn't want to fall in love with Ford, but she certainly wasn't ready to let him go. She'd enjoyed their superficial dating, each of them content to maintain the status quo and never pushing for more. An engagement, fake or not, was a huge step for a not-quite couple. Maybe too huge.

She blew out a breath and leaned against the arm of the sofa. "I need to think about this."

"Of course." He sat up, leaning forward so that she caught a hint of that sophisticated scent she'd come to enjoy so much.

"When do you need an answer?"

"I'd love to give you all the time you need, but I have to let the team know as soon as possible. We'll need time to plan a proposal, if you agree. If not, I'll have to move onto meeting the candidates. With so little time left to turn things around, I have to make my move soon."

She blew out a long breath, her cheeks puffing out. "Tell you what. Let me sleep on it, and I'll have an answer for you tomorrow." Given all the time in the world, she wouldn't be able to decide if this was brilliant or the stupidest idea ever. No need to draw it out too long.

His eyes lit up, and she wondered again why she was even considering this crazy scheme, encouraging him when it was clearly ridiculous. It probably said a lot about her that she was willing to entertain a political engagement, but the idea of opening herself up for a real relationship was out of the question. Getting engaged to Ford at this point in their relationship was absurd, but it did seem like a great way to protect herself from getting hurt. No real commitment, no real pain. As she often did when things were tough, she looked to the framed picture of a handsome soldier sitting on the shelf of her bar next to the bottle of Jack Daniels that sat unopened, waiting for someone who was never coming home.

•••

After tossing and turning all night, unable to sleep, Lily poured herself a glass of water and carried her laptop into the living room. The only way she'd be able to make her decision would be to hash it out with her best friend. She'd held off, thinking she could work it out on her own, because of Ford's need for secrecy. Carly wouldn't be checking email while on her honeymoon, but she'd feel better if she made the connection at least. Maybe writing out the message would make it clear, either that getting engaged was a good idea or that she had finally lost her mind. The more she thought about it, the more she wanted to say yes. If she could only talk it through, she'd know for sure what she wanted to do. Surely Carly could be trusted to keep the news to herself until they had a public engagement. She pulled her silky robe tighter around her body and settled on the floor in front of her coffee table. The screen lit up as she folded her long legs in front of her and sipped the ice-cold water. The handsome soldier smiled at her from his spot on the bar shelf, and her breath hitched.

Lily had married PFC Nathan Price against her parents' advice, right before she graduated from college, and spent one beautiful month as his wife before he deployed to Iraq. She'd sent him off to war, holding tight to his promise to return, and made do with emails, letters, and video chats while he was away. Less than eight months after their wedding, Nathan was killed by an IED while on a mission and Lily became a widow. At twenty-one.

The months after that fateful afternoon when two uniformed officers from the United States Army knocked on her door and changed her life had passed in a haze. Periods of disbelief mingled with the distinct sensation of everything leaning sideways, leaving Lily wondering if it was really all that important that she hang on. At a time when her friends were busy finishing college, getting jobs, and moving on with the next phase in their lives, Lily was mourning her husband, gone at least fifty years too soon.

Now she had to decide whether or not to do it again. Only this time, there would be no deployment or heartbreak, but no all-consuming love either. Nathan would want her to move on and find someone else, to tuck him away in her heart and fall in love again. She was certain he wouldn't want her to pass up the chance to be happy. He would've been so sad to know how long her depression lasted, how much of herself was lost when he died, how she'd let her life pass by without making another connection. What would he think of how much she'd changed? If he hadn't been killed, she'd be an army wife now, living on post, maybe working, maybe not. Without a doubt, her purpose would be supporting his career and raising the family they would've started. She wouldn't have become a model, and the only world traveling she'd have done would've been to army bases when he received his orders. And she would've loved it, all of it. If he'd lived, she'd be

Lily Price, wife and mother, not Lily Ashton, model and nobody special.

She shot off a quick email to Carly:

Hope you're having a beautiful time on your honeymoon! Give Michael a big hug for me, and be sure to eat lots of crepes and macarons on my behalf. I can't wait for you to get back home because things are crazy here. This sounds crazy, but Ford kind of proposed tonight. I haven't said yes or no, and you can't breathe a word of this to anyone. I wish you were here to talk it over with me so I could tell if I'm going crazy or not. I've been going over it all night, and I just can't decide. I told him I'd give him an answer tomorrow, which is way too soon, but I didn't want to make him wait too long. Love you, and see you soon.—Lil.

As soon as she pressed "send," everything became very real, as though putting it in writing made it official. Now that she'd told Carly, saying yes was almost inevitable. She couldn't let her friend in on the news and then turn Ford down. He'd be forced to propose to one of the fiancée candidates, and their secret would be out. Unless Carly helped her realize that she'd be making a huge mistake, this was happening. A handsome, important man who treated her well and made her feel amazing had proposed, sort of, and she'd promised an answer by the next day. Most people wouldn't consider this a recipe for a great marriage, but most people didn't lose their husbands while they were still newlyweds. Maybe this was just what she needed to find herself again, to open up to a little happiness. She didn't love Ford and he didn't love her, but there was no reason that couldn't develop over time. Besides, all he was asking for was an engagement. She could reserve marriage for if and when something real developed between them. It probably wouldn't, because Nathan took up too much space in her heart, but she'd worry about that after the election.

Her instant message notification pinged.

Carly: What do you mean, he "kind of" proposed???

Lily: What are you doing answering emails on your honeymoon?

Carly: It's 10 am here, and Michael went out to get croissants. Don't get me started on that man's unhealthy obsession with French pastries, and don't worry about what I'm doing—this is huge! I only have a few minutes before he gets back, so don't change the subject. I want to hear everything.

Lily: I guess I should change that to he proposed, no "kind of" about it. I told him I needed to think about it and would have an answer for him tomorrow. I've been thinking about it, of course I can't think about anything else, but I can't decide. Hence the late night message. Ugh—why aren't you here?

Carly: I know! Of all times to jet off to Paris! LOL. So, he proposed, out of the blue, and wasn't totally let down that you asked him for time to think about it?

Lily: That about sums it up. This whole thing is so weird.

Carly: What are you going to do?

Lily: I don't know! I kind of wish I hadn't said I'd give him an answer tomorrow. I didn't think we were there yet, but I do like him. A lot. We have a great time together, and I don't want to lose him. I'm afraid that if I say no, then we'll be finished. I don't think most guys stick around long after you turn down their proposals.

Carly: Did he seem super let down when you said you needed time to think about it? It sounds so exciting and romantic that he proposed out of the blue like that.

Lily: He couldn't have been more understanding. As soon as I hesitated, he told me to take all the time I need.

Carly: See, Ford's a good guy, Lil. You deserve to be happy, and I can tell that he cares about you. If you want to say yes, then what's stopping you?

Lily: You know.

Carly: Nathan?

Lily: Of course.

Carly: *Sigh* I know it's hard, but Nathan would want you to live your life. Everyone who knew you two could see that he loved you more than anything. If this is what you want, I know in my heart that he'd want this for you. He wouldn't expect you to mourn him forever. In fact, he'd probably be so sad to see that you're having such a hard time without him. It's okay to move on, truly. It doesn't mean you've forgotten him, and it definitely doesn't make what you had together any less important. Nobody would expect you to stay single forever, least of all Nathan.

Lily: I've told myself the same thing, but it's still so hard. I know he'd hate to see how long I've been in this holding pattern. Ford is a good guy, but don't you don't think the whole thing sounds a bit sounds crazy? I mean, we haven't even slept together yet.

Carly: It's unexpected, but I wouldn't say it's crazy. You guys are old enough to know what you want and recognize a good thing when it comes your way. I'll even bet that if you ask nicely Ford will oblige you with some sexy time. I can think of worse husbands than a sophisticated and handsome congressman, LOL.

Lily: True. He'd be a good husband. Smart, charming, good citizen, and all that.

Carly: Not to mention ridiculously good looking.

Lily: Yes, there's that too. Thanks for the talk. I think I know what I'm going to do. Don't say anything to anyone, not even Michael. I don't want word getting out until I talk to Ford.

Carly: My lips are sealed!

Lily: Thank you. I wish you were here, and I miss you!!

Carly: I miss you too. See you next week.

She could chat with Carly all night and still come to the same conclusion, no matter what arguments she brought up. The simple fact was that she had to decide this one herself. Whether it was the late hour or the fact that Carly was so supportive, Lily didn't know, but saying yes to Ford's proposal seemed like a good idea. Sure, she hadn't been able to tell Carly the whole truth, but the parts she'd shared had been absolutely true. She'd return to the world of the living without being forced to open herself up to real love and the potential heartbreak that came with it. They made a good team, and the engagement would be good for her. Publicity-wise, it might help bring some attention to Soldier On and bring her that much closer to realizing her dream. He was a clean politician with a solid record who was well-regarded in the state. What more could she ask for? Her one true love had come and gone already. This wasn't exactly second chance at blissful happiness, but it was close. And close was fine with Lily.

Tomorrow, she'd say yes.

Chapter Five

The next morning, after stumbling through his morning routine like a zombie, unable to think of anything but how Lily would answer his proposal, Ford pulled into the campaign headquarters parking lot. Before he even reached his car after leaving her apartment last night he wondered what had gotten into him. They were nowhere near ready for marriage. She must think he was delusional. He sat in his car, enjoying the last moments of solitude before facing his team at their morning meeting. Joelle's car was in the lot already, and staffers and volunteers were filtering into his campaign headquarters, but he wasn't ready to go in yet. He'd have to put off the discussion about potential fiancées once he went in since he didn't know what Lily was going to say, and he hated stalling.

He laughed to himself, thinking if he were a better politician, it would all be easier to talk his way around it without giving a real answer. The team was expecting a decision, or to at least schedule the meetings with the women, but he wanted to hold out for Lily's answer. What had he been thinking, asking her to agree to this? He was lucky she hadn't kicked him out once she discovered he was no different than any other politician, that appearances were all that mattered. When it came down to it, he hadn't been able to let her go without at least asking. Granted, they weren't ready for the next step in their relationship, but he sure as hell wasn't ready to cut ties and say goodbye forever. But if he were going to have a public political engagement, maybe it was best to keep emotions out of it, focus on the business arrangement that it was. Maybe he should leave Lily out of it, let her be free to find someone who wasn't an idiot whose life decisions were made by a committee.

His phone buzzed on the seat beside him, ending his mental self-flagellation. It was Lily. This was it, the moment he'd been waiting for. Before it could go to voicemail, he answered the phone.

"Hey, you." Good, his voice was steady, easy, not like his heart was stuck in his throat.

"Hey." Lily's voice was a ribbon of smooth warmth, sending his pulse racing at a mad gallop. "So, I thought about it, all night, and I talked to Carly." She paused, sending his heart plummeting into his gut. Nobody could know about the engagement scheme! "Don't worry, I didn't tell her that you had to propose for your campaign, although I'm sure she could keep a secret for me. I just told her you proposed." Relief flooded him, making him realize how nervous he'd been not only about Lily's answer but about the possibility of his secret being revealed.

"And?" If he had to wait for her answer much longer, his heart might actually beat out of his chest.

She didn't answer right away, and he couldn't breathe. "I'm in."

He exhaled and hit the steering wheel with his open hand in triumph. "Yes! Thank you!"

She laughed, the most melodic sound he'd ever heard. "I guess you're happy."

He couldn't wipe the giant smile off his face if he wanted to. "Hell yes, I'm happy. Thank you, Lily. Thank you so much. I've been sitting in the parking lot, dreading my morning meeting because I was afraid they'd want me to look at the file folder women again. I can't tell you how happy you've made me."

"I'm glad to help. Anything to save you from the binder full of women." He could hear the indulgence in her voice and pictured her full lips turned up in a smile.

"Are you free tonight? I want to make it official." His mind turned with possibilities for their engagement. He'd treat her to something special, something nice to thank her for signing on for this crazy task.

"Sure, I guess there's no time like the present."

"Great. I've got some ideas, and I'll take care of everything." Ford turned his car off and stepped out into the parking lot, suddenly lighter. "I'll set everything up and will call you this afternoon with the details. Thanks again, Lily."

"You're welcome. See you tonight."

He ended the call and forced himself to appear calm and normal as he approached the headquarters office. Campaign posters lined the glass windows of the storefront, urging people to *Re-Elect FORD RICHARDSON* and *Stand Strong with FORD*. For the first time in a while, he thought they might have a chance to win this thing. So many obstacles had sprung up along his road to re-election, but with the engagement locked down, the path was clear again. Opening the door to the buzz of activity—staffers chatting, volunteers manning the phone bank, copiers printing—was exhilarating. Once the engagement was settled, the work this office did on his behalf would be more effective, with the issue of his bachelor status put to rest.

As he cut through the sea of activity swirling around the campaign headquarters, he greeted staffers as he passed, shaking hands, patting shoulders, offering hearty thanks. To them, it probably seemed like he was well-rested and ready to take on the week. Nobody knew yet that the tides were about to shift, that the campaign was about to take off. He'd save the celebration dance for behind closed doors, but he did allow himself one quick fist in the air, raised in victory, as he approached the conference room.

"Good morning, everyone." He greeted the team and took his seat, not trying to hide his excitement. He knew he was smiling like an idiot, but he didn't care.

"Good morning, Ford. I'd ask how you are, but it's pretty clear that you're terribly depressed. What's got you down?" Charlie Tibbals teased.

"Well, I'm getting engaged tonight." With a satisfied smile, he leaned back in his chair and watched for their reactions.

Robert leaned on an elbow, clicking his pen. "How? We haven't even scheduled the fiancée candidate meetings, much less chosen the lucky bride."

"Forget the fake fiancées." He eyed the stack of file folders on the corner of the table and wished he could push them into the garbage can. "I've discussed our situation with the woman I'm seeing, and she's agreed to take things to the next level." He held up a hand, ready to stop objections before they were voice. "Don't worry. This is legit, not some political maneuvering or anything." That wasn't entirely true, of course, but it was close enough. She may have agreed to the engagement with full knowledge of the situation, but there was at least a basis for their relationship, which was more than he could say for any of the team's pre-screened candidates. Keeping the secret between Lily and himself minimized the possibility that the truth would slip out, too. The last thing he wanted was to potentially humiliate her after she'd agreed to help him out. "She accepted my private proposal this morning, and we'll have a public engagement this evening."

While he'd hoped for a more enthusiastic reaction, Ford knew that his taking matters into his own hands was not in their plans. They insisted on running a tight ship, and their many successes with dozens of other campaigns justified their pride. "I'm sorry to spring it on you, but the more I thought about it, the more I realized I didn't want to end things with her to start a fake relationship with one of the ladies you found for me. We've been seeing each other for quite a while, and things are going well. It moves our personal timetable up quite a bit, but we just couldn't say goodbye to each other."

"Well now, don't keep us waiting," Charlie began slowly, and Ford could imagine the gears shifting in his head as they changed course. They liked to be in charge, but they were also highly adaptable. "Who is she?"

Besides his savior? "Her name is Lily Ashton, and we've been dating for the last several months."

"She's the one who always shows up to events with you, right?" Robert asked.

"That's the one. She's a model, and she's a college graduate, no kids, no criminal history that I know of, always perfectly at ease in front of the camera, of course. I think she'll be a great asset to the campaign as well. Basically, she's the perfect woman."

Robert pushed off his elbow, sitting up straighter as he processed the news. "People have seen you two together, so it might not come as huge surprise. This could work. Might even be easier to pull off than bringing in a stranger and asking people to buy it. If nothing else, it'll save time."

"Well," Charlie said, crossing off a line from his agenda with a quick stroke of his pen. "I guess that's settled, then. If your bride to be is amenable to having the engagement public, then I don't think we have anything more to discuss. I'll get the press release drafted, and we'll have it ready after the big moment. Does Joelle have your itinerary? She can arrange for a photographer and make sure there's some press."

"She doesn't, but I'll make sure she does when we finalize our plans. I haven't decided exactly where we'll do it, but we are set for tonight." He'd solved a major issue facing his campaign, but he was the only one excited about the progress. Going for it and asking Lily to team up was a smart move. His team saw procurement of a fiancée as a line item on the weekly agenda, and he would've been the only one suffering had they chosen a stranger from the list of candidates. This way he at least got to pair up with a woman he liked.

The rest of the meeting flew by in a barrage of information, meeting notes, appearance requests, and poll results. Ford's re-election was riding on the information they threw at him, but his mind was on Lily. With the time he'd freed up by eliminating the fiancée candidate interviews, he could shop for her engagement ring and make arrangements for the official proposal. He'd presented it as an agreement, a political move, but there was no reason he couldn't surprise her, try to make her happy in the process. She may not realize it yet, but she was doing him a huge favor, and he wouldn't forget that. She deserved something nice, something that fit what he hoped would be their growing relationship. During election season, everything was focused on him, his platform, his stats, his chances. It was fun to think of someone else for a change. And if that someone else was 5'10" with endless legs and the face of an angel, then so much the better.

•••

Lily sat on her bed, feet tucked under a fuzzy pink blanket and stared at her phone. She could put it off all she wanted, but eventually she was going to have to call her parents and tell them about her upcoming engagement. Saying yes to Ford's proposal was easy enough, but her parents were probably going to be a bit more difficult to handle. Risking them finding out after the fact was unacceptable, so she dialed their number, hoping to catch them at home together. She held her breath as the phone rang, not sure if she wanted them to answer or not.

"Hi, honey." Her dad picked up after a couple of rings.

"Hi, Dad. Is Mom home?" She leaned back against her pillows, twisting the end of her ponytail around her fingers.

"Sure, is everything okay?" The concern in her father's voice made her wish she didn't have to break the news.

"Yes, everything's fine. I just need to talk to both of you."

The wait for her mother to pick up the phone was interminable. For everything that she'd been through, Lily felt foolish for being afraid to talk to her own parents, but there was almost no way they'd be pleased with what she was about to tell them.

"Hi, Lil." Her mother's soft voice came on the line, and Lily took a deep breath.

"I wanted to talk to you guys together because I have some exciting news." She pressed her lips together, willing her voice to stop shaking. She was an adult making her own decision, and there was nothing to fear. Trying to inject as much confidence and enthusiasm as she could into her voice, she continued. "I'm getting married."

Silence filled the line, making it impossible for Lily to gauge her parents' reaction. Finally, her mother spoke. "To whom?"

They hadn't met Ford, but they knew about him. "To Ford, of course. I haven't been seeing anyone else."

"So, you're engaged to a congressman?" Her father finally found his voice.

"Yes, Dad. That's the one."

"Oh, honey, that's great." The disappointment in his voice cut through his words.

"We'll have a long engagement, so you'll get a chance to get to know him. I just wanted to let you know because we're going public with the engagement soon, and, of course, I wanted you to hear it from me." They weren't thrilled, but maybe the call would be easier than she'd anticipated.

After a pause, her father spoke again. "Is it that you're worried you won't find anyone else?"

"What? No! Why would you say that?"

"Sweetheart, it just seems to me that a Republican congressman is the last person you would choose to be your husband. Aren't you worried about Soldier On?"

"Of course I am, but Ford has nothing to do with that."

"Sweetheart, any husband can help or hurt your efforts, but I'm more worried when that husband is a conservative politician.

I'm sure he won't try to make things harder for us, but I can't see him being much help towards reaching your goals. That's all I'm saying."

"It feels like you're saying that he's not who *you* would choose. *You* don't know anything about him." Lily surprised herself with the protectiveness she felt toward Ford and their relationship.

Her dad sighed. "I'm sorry I brought it up. I guess I just worry about you so much. It's true that if I had my choice, it would be someone who is a little more used to caring about social issues and other people."

"Ted, we don't know that he doesn't care about people. That's a pretty big assumption to make." Her mother finally spoke.

"I know Republicans, Jules. And they don't exactly mix well with the kind of progressive social change we work toward. Honey, I hope he proves me wrong. I really do."

Ford had been nothing but supportive of her work with Soldier On, had even offered to help her get the word out. The only way she'd know if he was sincere would be to give it time, though. He'd have to come through with the interview or show her in other ways that he was interested in their success. She knew going into the engagement that they would have detractors, so facing her parents was likely the first of many times she'd have to defend their relationship.

"Obviously, I hope you'll support us, but if you don't feel that you can, that's your choice."

"Sweetheart, we do support you. We love you, and we'd love to meet Ford. Bring him by the house, okay?" Her mother jumped in, likely worried that her dad's judgment would cause a rift.

They had been summarily opposed to her first engagement, and it was ages before their relationship was repaired. She'd married Nathan despite their protests, and when he died, it was harder for them to come together in grief. They had argued that not only was she too young to get married, but that army life was tough, that her marriage would be more stressful for the deployments. They worried that his job was too dangerous, that he'd be sent into combat. They had no idea how right they were, and it lingered between them, an unspoken awkward reminder, when they came together as a family after his death.

"Sure. I know he'd like to meet you, too."

She ended the call with her parents, sorry that tension was rising up again just when she and her father were getting along so well. Working together on Soldier On had brought them closer, had allowed them to get to know one another in a new light. She hated to threaten the easy rapport they'd developed, but she couldn't keep her engagement a secret. She'd agreed, and the only thing left was to make it official.

• • •

What did one wear to a real proposal from a not-quite boyfriend for a political engagement that might not last past November? Lily stood in front of her closet that evening, scanning the selection and wishing she'd had more notice so she could shop for the perfect outfit. Though to be fair, she had more clothes than one person could ever wear, and nothing could quell her nerves as she waited for Ford. Except for maybe Ford himself. Once he arrived, and she could look into his eyes, she'd breathe again, confident she'd made the right decision and ready to move forward. She slipped on a simple red sheath that ended right above the knees, the color a nod to his political affiliation, and pushed her feet into the black Louboutin stilettos she'd worn to Carly's wedding. Swiveling in front of her mirror, she admired the sassy bows on the backs of the shoes and remembered how Ford's eyes had been drawn to her bare legs more than once the other night. Satisfied with her appearance, she tucked essentials into her clutch and went to the living room to wait.

As punctual as he was handsome, Ford arrived at her apartment at six o'clock sharp. At the sound of his knock, her heart raced, pounding in her chest. With a shaking hand, she grabbed her clutch and somehow managed to propel herself across the apartment to let him in. He stood in the doorway, almost shockingly handsome in a charcoal tailored suit and looking as nervous as she felt.

"Hi." She whispered the word, knowing she sounded ridiculous but unable to pull herself together.

"Hi." The tension broke with his smile, and she breathed him in. That sophisticated bergamot scent that both enticed and relaxed her, the perfectly Ford combination of elements. "It looks like you're ready to go."

"Yep. I was nervous when I was waiting for you. This is a big deal, you know, but I'm ready now." Nervous didn't begin to describe it, but every second she stood beside him, the anxiety subsided.

His eyes crinkled at the corners when he smiled. "I'm glad you didn't change your mind."

"Of course not. I wouldn't want you to have to resort to the file folder women." She shuddered dramatically and was rewarded with Ford's rich laughter. Making the joke lightened the situation, reminded her that this was going to be fun.

"You saved me from a hideous fate," he said with a grin. "Shall we?" He stepped toward the door, clearly looking forward to the evening.

Lily had worried that he might want to know more about her first marriage now that they were getting engaged, that there would at least be questions. He knew all the basics, but she hadn't elaborated more than absolutely necessary in their past conversations. Nathan occupied so much of her heart, but she wanted to keep as much of their life together as possible to herself. The more she talked about him, the more real his death seemed. Ford didn't seem to have any concerns or questions, though, which was a relief. Lily didn't like talking about Nathan with people who didn't know him. It was too painful, so Ford's lack of curiosity was refreshing. And why should he be bothered? They were about to embark on an engagement brought on by necessity, not a real commitment blossoming from their deep and abiding love for one another. There was no reason for him to complicate matters with a lot of unnecessary discussion about past romances or comparisons. She certainly didn't know much about his romantic history. It was best this way, less likely that they'd get hurt. Their relationship was surface-level and their engagement was a practicality, and she should keep that in mind. Her first marriage was real, so real she sometimes didn't recognize that it was truly over. Keeping the two separate was a lot easier than figuring out how to open her heart to someone new.

She locked up behind her and took his offered hand as they walked out of her building. Warmth traveled up her arm as he entwined his fingers with hers, sending a bloom of excitement through her. Staged engagement or not, it was going to be a fun and romantic evening. A perfect gentleman, Ford let her into the passenger seat of his car before getting in himself. As he navigated out of the parking lot, she adjusted the air conditioning vents to face her.

"By the way, I told my parents that you proposed, so they won't be surprised when the engagement becomes public. I have good news and bad news." She checked her makeup in the visor mirror.

He glanced at her before turning his attention back to the early evening traffic. "Give me the good news."

"They think I'm crazy to do this, but they promise to be supportive and keep their opinions to themselves."

"About me?"

"About everything. Me getting married again, especially to someone they've never met. It's a bit much for them to take in, but they've promised to be supportive." She wasn't sure how supportive they would be, but she felt confident that they would at least give him a chance.

He turned onto the highway and shot her a quick grin. "That sounds great so far; I mean, we couldn't really ask for more. What's the bad news?"

"They want to meet you, and they don't exactly vote Republican." That was an understatement, but he'd find that out soon enough.

"That doesn't sound so bad. Sounds completely reasonable, actually, and I'm great with parents. Don't worry about it. I won't hold their politics against them." She had to laugh at his easy confidence; he had no idea who he was dealing with. It would be interesting to watch, at least.

"I'm more worried about their opinion about your politics, actually. They are firm in their beliefs, and it won't be easy." She shrugged. "Meeting the parents, all the nerves, it's completely normal, but given the circumstances…"

"Yet another reason it's good that we are the only two who know that there are, in fact, circumstances. Can you imagine trying to explain to your parents that I needed a fiancée and you agreed to take the job?"

The laugh that escaped was so abrupt it was almost a snort. "Ha! I can't even tell you how crazy that would be." Their disdain of politicians, especially conservatives, combined with this scheme? Their heads might explode. "It would confirm everything they think they know about politicians."

"Will your father be insulted that I didn't ask his permission?"

Not likely, since the last time she got engaged, she'd ignored their pleas to reconsider and plowed ahead with her plans. They thought she was too young for marriage, that starting her married life off with her husband leaving on a long deployment was foolish, that she should wait until he returned home. She hadn't listened, and they didn't attend the City Hall nuptials, creating a huge rift between them that only widened as she adjusted to her life as a newlywed with a husband at war. After their conversation that morning, if they ever tried to stop her from getting married again, Lily would be surprised.

"No, he and my mom are very comfortable with my independence. They just want to get to know you, which I now realize will be strange if they start to think of you as part of the family and we don't end up getting married after the election. I didn't think of it until just now, but people will expect us to set a date and start planning the wedding. I haven't thought further than the engagement! I don't know how long I can put my mom and Carly off before I have to start looking at venues and wedding dresses." She gripped the door handle, thinking for the first time that this fake engagement might backfire on her. The idea that she could walk away if she wanted when November rolled around was her security blanket and had apparently blinded her to the details. Was she going to find herself trapped in a fake marriage? "Crap. What am I going to do?"

Ford put his hand on her thigh and rubbed gently, the warmth and weight of it melting her stress again. Had he always had this calming influence on her? Maybe that's why she gravitated toward him. "Let's take it one step at a time. We can tell people that we want a long engagement and we're going to put off even thinking about wedding planning until after the election. I'm sure it will make perfect sense to everyone. Then the holidays will be a distraction, and before you know it, six months will have gone by and then we can worry about it again. If you're still willing."

She relaxed against the buttery soft leather of the seat and let the relief sink in. "You're absolutely right. I don't know why I didn't think of that."

"It's good that you brought it up. Better to anticipate any possible complications than to be surprised and blow our cover. Tonight, try to relax and have fun. My assistant arranged for a photographer to catch the moment I propose, so don't let that surprise you. Tomorrow morning, my team will send out a press release, and then the real work will begin."

"It sounds so romantic," she joked. "A press release and me trying my best to look surprised when you propose."

"Hey, just because you know it's coming tonight doesn't mean you know when. I'll keep some of the details to myself so you won't have to act shocked."

"Sounds like you've thought of everything." She settled back in her seat and tried to relax.

Ford exited the freeway and negotiated traffic through the one-way streets of downtown Dallas. Lily watched the city roll by in a wave of lights and movement as they made their way to the Dallas Museum of Art. They'd stroll through the space, take in the current exhibitions and the permanent collections, make small talk, and then her life would change. Lily's knee bounced up and down as he found a spot in the parking garage, until Ford's hand stilled her.

"Try to relax." His easy smile sent warmth through her that calmed her nerves. "The hard part was making the decision, so let me handle everything tonight. This is going to be fun."

He was right. They were embarking on an exciting adventure together, one she'd readily agreed to, and she should enjoy it. They'd spend a nice evening together, share a moment, and get on with it. They always had fun together, never had even the smallest disagreement. Sure, that was probably due to the fact that everything between them was strictly casual up until now, but this engagement wouldn't likely change much between them. They'd see each other more often, and they'd share a giant secret, but their relationship wouldn't change. With a shared goal of presenting a united front, all Lily had to do was relax and enjoy the public affection of a sexy man who made her laugh and kept things interesting.

The museum was typically closed at five, but members were invited to the opening of a special Manet and Cezanne exhibit that evening, and excitement was in the air. Patrons wandered through the space, murmuring and pausing in front of priceless pieces of art. Lily's shoes clicked on the polished floor, and she tucked her hand into the crook of Ford's arm, leaning close as they stopped in front of Monet's *Water Lilies*, a painting she'd seen a dozen times before but always loved. The soothing scene of soft lilies floating in blue and green waters brought her to a simpler, calmer time. She dropped her head onto his shoulder, loving that he was tall enough for her to do so.

"It's beautiful, isn't it?" His baritone rumbled through her.

"Mmm hmm. I've always loved this piece." The painting had been part of the museum's permanent collection since she could remember, and ever since her first visit during a high school field trip, she'd been drawn to it. The lazy, filtered picture was so relaxing and soothing.

"I never get tired of being able to walk in here and see an actual Monet, but I still enjoy the Kandinskys a little more."

"Really?" She couldn't believe anyone would prefer the hard lines and bright colors of Kandinsky over the dreamy, muted tones of Monet.

"I think it reminds me of when I was a kid and thought the more modern paintings were so cool. My parents dragged me and my brothers to museums constantly, and I didn't exactly appreciate it then. When we were boys, we just tried to find something that looked interesting so we wouldn't die of boredom. We weren't exactly allowed to complain."

The thought of little Rutherford Richardson and his brothers forced to quietly wander through art museums, hands shoved in their pockets or tucked behind their backs, was precious. Lily pictured a smaller version of him, the same amazing blue eyes, lit up with mischief, under a mop of brown hair. He probably wore little suits, too. Adorable. Did Ford want kids of his own? Did she? *Whoa, Lily. One thing at a time. Let's get engaged first.* They wandered further into the gallery until Ford stopped in front of a Georgia O'Keeffe painting and examined it, stroking his chin thoughtfully.

She slapped his arm playfully. "Stop it. You cannot propose to me in front of this painting."

"Hey, this is a painting of a flower. I don't know what you see in it, but maybe you need to get your mind out of the gutter." He took her hand and continued through the museum, cracking up at his own joke about the artist's suggestive imagery.

The museum housed an incredible collection of ancient Mediterranean pieces, and they stopped in front of a solid gold Greek wreath dating back to the fourth century B.C.

"It's amazing, isn't it?" Lily took in the beautifully preserved details of the wreath, awestruck that something so old was sitting in front of her, just like that. "Have you seen this piece before?"

Ford didn't answer, and she turned to find him kneeling beside her, hope and affection in his blue eyes. He pulled a little blue Tiffany box from his jacket's interior pocket and flipped the top open. A stunning princess cut solitaire flanked by smaller channel set diamonds on a thick platinum band was nestled in the velvet fold of the box, and her hands flew to her lips. It was perfect.

"Oh, wow." It was all she could manage. This moment was planned and seamlessly orchestrated, and it wasn't exactly authentic, but the emotions flooding her certainly were.

"Lily Ashton, you are the most amazing person I know. When I'm with you, everything is better, and I don't want to spend another day without knowing that you'll be my wife. Will you marry me?" Ford's voice caught on the last word.

"Yes," she whispered, nodding, and he slipped the ring on her finger. Catching his face in her hands as he rose, their lips met in a sweet, hopeful kiss. His lips were warm, and she could taste the slightest hint of cinnamon. Perfect. With a quick lift, Ford picked her up, and she laughed against his lips as her feet kicked lightly behind her. He set her down, gently so she didn't topple over off the four-inch heels, and pressed another kiss to her forehead as his arms tightened around her. His strong embrace was brief, but for one perfect moment, she let herself believe she'd made the right decision.

"She said yes!" he said with a huge smile to the curious onlookers around them.

A small crowd had gathered when he dropped to his knee and erupted in applause at his exclamation. Lily wiped a tear from her cheek and accepted a warm kiss on her temple from her fiancé. The photographer she hadn't noticed before asked for the couple to pose, and they threw matching radiant smiles his way as Ford wrapped her in his arms. This was practically a business transaction, nothing more, and she knew that. Ford needed a fiancée, and Lily needed an escape from hiding from something real. Her heart overflowed, though, because it was sincere, as sincere as it could be in their situation, and it was enough. He hadn't professed a love she knew wasn't genuine; he'd chosen his words carefully, so that every part of his proposal was heartfelt and true. Ford kissed her temple again, and she turned to catch his lips with hers. With the audience not quite dispersed, they shared a chaste kiss, perfect for the camera. The way he pulled her close, one hand on the back of her head, promised more to come. After months of dating with little more than a few heated kisses, Lily was ready for something more to happen.

As though reading her mind, Ford grabbed her hand and led her through the elegant crowd as quickly as he could without dragging her. Light caught on the facets of the diamond resting on her ring finger, and the weight of what she'd agreed to pulled at the corner of her exhilaration with every step across the glossy marble floor. One look at the man at her side brushed aside the doubts simmering below the surface, at least for the moment. This was perfect, the two of them. Beautiful chemistry, and easy back and forth, but no illusions of some great love. The ideal situation for someone who didn't have a heart to give away anymore.

Their footsteps and hushed laughter echoed through the empty parking garage as they found Ford's car. Instead of letting her in on the passenger side, he flashed a wicked grin and opened the back door for her to climb in. Not even in their giddy state would they actually have sex in a public place, but Lily knew the darkened garage and the car's tinted windows would hide whatever mischief they got up to. She slid in and toed her shoes off onto the floor mat. With a slam of the door, Ford joined her, and they were alone, blissfully alone.

"I wanted a moment of privacy with my new fiancée." He grinned, and her insides turned to jelly. Somehow with the engagement now official, it was safe to let down some of the resistance she naturally threw up against her attraction to him. The boundaries they'd agreed upon erased the compulsion to hold back for fear of Ford not reciprocating.

"I didn't realize there would be a ring," she blurted, realizing how stupid she sounded as soon as the words were out of her mouth. "I mean, I should've guessed, but all I thought about was the proposal. That was a nice touch."

Ford's easy laugh wound around her in the small space. "We can't very well get engaged without a ring. I hope you like it; I wanted to have at least some part of this be a surprise for you."

She admired the huge diamond resting on her finger, figuring it at least two and a half if not three carats. Yeah, it would do. "I love it, Ford. It's truly exquisite."

He shrugged, though he looked pleased that she was happy with it. "I thought it suited you. A beautiful ring for a stunning woman."

"You're sweet." She breathed him in and watched as he loosened his tie and undid the top few buttons of his shirt. The intense gleam in his eyes was anything but sweet, and an answering need welled inside her.

Without further thought, she urged him closer to her, gently but insistently, by softly tugging the tie he'd loosened. Capturing his lips with hers, Ford pulled her up to straddle his lap and moved to the center of the backseat in one smooth motion. At almost six feet tall, Lily always felt Amazonian, but in Ford's arms, she felt light, protected, and utterly feminine. He coaxed her lips open to deepen the kiss, their tongues tangling as her fitted sheath dress rode up her thighs. His arms snaked around her, pulling her closer as she fitted herself against him. Ford buried his face against her neck, sending hot breath and electric shivers across her skin. He nipped at the sensitive spot between her neck and shoulder, dropping quick kisses as he nudged the fabric off of her shoulder. As his lips worked their magic, his hands slid down her back to cup her butt. He pulled her tighter against him, gently rocking her against the indisputable evidence of his arousal. His grip tightened, the pace quickened, and he moved from her neck to her ear.

"God, Lily, you're so gorgeous," he whispered. "I want you so bad." He worked a hand beneath her until he could slip inside the thin fabric of her tiny lace panties. She didn't even try to suppress the gasp that escaped her lips as his expert fingers went to work. He inhaled deeply as he kissed the spot behind her ear. "You smell incredible."

Things were getting out of hand, going too far. She stiffened in his embrace, afraid to say anything but unable to recover her carefree mood. A slight tremble shook her body as she realized what she'd agreed to with the engagement and how far she'd almost gone in the backseat of the car.

"What's wrong?" His voice broke through the silence, blessedly sounding worried instead of aggravated, and she couldn't hide from him. She peeled her eyes open with great effort, to see genuine concern in his expression. Ford ran his hands up and down her sides, calming her.

She shook her head. "I'm sorry. I got carried away, and I don't think I can do this." As the words spilled out of her mouth, she cringed. Carried away was putting it mildly. She'd ground herself against him like a horny teenager, in a car where anyone could walk by and take a peek. She'd led him on without even stopping to think about the consequences. "I can't believe I did that. I haven't been with anyone since my husband died, and I'm not ready. I'm sorry, really, because I should have thought about that before all this started." She waved her hand weakly between them, trying to explain.

"Hey, it's okay. We don't have to do anything you don't want to do." The worry in his voice softened to understanding. "This is a lot for one day, and I don't mind waiting. We can take things slow."

She slipped off his lap, pulling her dress down over her thighs as she moved, and sat beside him in the backseat, sighing softly as she slipped her feet back into her shoes. She couldn't believe how close she'd come to giving in to her attraction without even thinking through things first. It was bad enough that she'd agreed to marry someone else. She couldn't betray Nathan by developing genuine feelings for Ford, too. The raw exposure of giving him control over her like that was unnerving. The past several years had made Lily an expert at maintaining tight control over her emotions and desires, the best way she knew to guard her heart against shattering. She never let herself fall for anyone, and at the very least didn't enjoy a man more than he enjoyed her. Ford was working on breaking all her rules, and incredibly, she wasn't sure she'd try to stop him for much longer. She wasn't quite ready to cross that bridge, though.

"Tonight was supposed to be fun, and I'm sorry for ruining it. You put together such a nice proposal." She fiddled with the fabric of her dress, uncomfortable meeting his gaze. "Maybe we should call it a night."

Ford shifted in the seat beside her. "Sure, sure, no problem. But Lily, really, you didn't ruin anything. This engagement is going to save my campaign, and I am incredibly grateful to you. I'm the one who got carried away, and I won't push you again."

They moved to the front seat in awkward silence before Ford pulled out of the parking garage and drove her home.

Chapter Six

Ford smiled to himself as he exited Central Expressway several miles before Lily thought he would. She'd given him directions to her parents' house, and he'd picked her up a bit early to surprise her with a quick side trip.

"Um, you know that wasn't our exit, right?"

Ford put his hand on her knee and squeezed, loving how natural it felt to reach out and touch her. "I've got a quick surprise first, if that's okay with you."

She grinned. "That sounds exciting."

He followed the directions Joelle had sent him and found the building. "Here we are."

Lily's brow furrowed in confusion as he unbuckled his seatbelt and opened the door. Ford walked around to her side and opened the door, offering his hand as she stepped out. She didn't need his help, but he was glad when she took it. Ford led her to the door of the nondescript commercial building.

Fishing a key out of his pocket, he opened the door and held it for her. "Let's check it out."

Lily stepped in, elegant in the bland environment. White walls, low pile gray carpet, and generic office furniture greeted them. The air was still and chilly, but the place was clean. She turned as she took in the space, and finally spoke up. "All right. I give up. What is this place?"

"This could potentially be Soldier On. Joelle's husband is a commercial real estate agent, and he is a genius at matching tenants and buildings. It's just an idea, of course. There are plenty of other spaces when you're ready to decide. He's available to meet up with you if you want, but I thought it would be fun to show you this place myself."

He could practically see the wheels turning as Lily walked around the building. "Oh my gosh. This would be perfect! It's got everything." She ran her hand lightly against the wall as they passed empty offices and found a kitchen. "I can't believe you had time to do this."

"Honestly, all I did was talk with Joelle's husband about your organization and what you had in mind. He did all the hard work. I'm happy to take credit though."

He pulled her close, pressing a soft kiss to her lips. "This was a nice surprise, Ford. Thank you."

"It was nothing. I can look at other spaces with you if you want, or I can turn you and your dad over to the real estate agent." He cringed. "Speaking of your dad, I guess we should get going. I'm sure they're expecting us."

• • •

"This is the part where you tell me not to worry because they'll love me." Ford pulled Lily's hand to stop her on the walkway leading toward her parents' front door. The suburban neighborhood buzzed with the sound of dogs and children outside enjoying the unseasonably warm fall temperature.

She squeezed his hand and grinned. "I would, but I'm not a liar."

He tossed his head back with a laugh. "Oh, great. I can't wait to meet them."

"They're…different. They may not adore you at first sight, but I'm sure they'll be polite. You have nothing, well, mostly nothing, to worry about." She bounced on her toes, adorable in the late-afternoon sunlight.

"You'd think I'd be used to venturing into hostile territory by now, but a congressional campaign is nothing compared to meeting the parents."

"They're outspoken, maybe even a little extreme in their views, but they stay out of my relationships." The cocked eyebrow told Ford that Lily had at least guessed that his family probably wouldn't approve of her, and at least she didn't have a seven-member advisory team passing judgment on him. "And they won't try to make you uncomfortable like some people would, so relax. Oh, and be sure to call them Ted and Jules."

"Fair enough. Let's get this party started."

Before Lily could knock or turn the knob, the door opened to reveal a thoroughly-average middle-aged couple who were clearly pleased to see their daughter. She leaned down to embrace them each in turn, their greetings lost against her shoulders. With his hands shoved into his pockets, Ford rocked back on his heels, waiting for an opening to approach the trio.

Lily's mother disentangled herself and enveloped Ford in a patchouli-scented hug, her sturdy, warm body against his a welcome change from the formal air kisses and brittle half-hearted embraces he received from his own mother. She ushered him inside, following Lily and her father.

"Come on in, you two. It's not every day we entertain a congressman." Jules encouraged them to sit in the living room while she bustled into the kitchen. Ted's grudgingly muttered greeting told Ford all he needed to know about how the couple's politics meshed with his own. If the lackluster reception wasn't enough of a clue, the pictures of the Ashtons either raising signs at protests or posing with well-known liberals and civil rights activists filled in the blanks. He had his work cut out for him.

Still, he didn't need their votes; he needed their support for the engagement. Barring that, he'd settle for getting out of the house without major incident. "So, Ted, Lily has told me a lot about the new organization you're starting. She said you're on the board."

"I am. It's been great working with her, and of course it's exciting to be on the ground floor of something that's shaping up to be so useful for the community." Ted looked like he could be persuaded to continue, and Ford was grateful to have found the safe conversation topic so quickly.

Jules came back in bearing a tray with glasses of ice and a pitcher of tea. "Sit and relax, Ford. Don't let Ted try to recruit you for anything." She laughed, sounding a lot like Lily, before setting the tray on the coffee table and taking a seat on the chair opposite Ted's while Ford and Lily sat on the sofa.

Ted scoffed. "I doubt anything we're doing is of interest to the congressman. Recruiting him would probably be impossible."

"Dad, come on," Lily said, her voice soft but chiding. "Be nice."

"Listen, I'm just saying, I have a hard time believing that Mr. Richardson here is interested in the work that we do. He's part of the same Congress that voted to cut military benefits and continues to ignore the growing troubles of service men and women returning to civilian life." He threw up his hands, disgusted. "It's like they're actively working against the men and women they send into these wars."

Ford accepted the glass of iced tea and sympathetic look from Jules and cleared his throat. He'd hoped to avoid getting involved in politics, but Ted wasn't going to allow it. "I understand why you'd be hesitant to believe that I care about or even understand the issues that you and Lily are confronted with when you see potential clients." He paused to sip from his glass. "But I've never once voted against a measure that would help our veterans or active military. I am interested in learning more, and I hope that I can use my connections and influence to help you and Lily with this venture. I really do."

Lily leaned closer and laid her hand on his thigh, her light perfume drifting towards him. "Ford knows the woman who books guests for *Good Morning, Dallas*, and he's put in a call to get us a spot." Her bright tone practically begged her father to drop his offensive and look on the bright side. "And, before we got here, we stopped at a potential space for Soldier On. Ford knows a great commercial real estate agent, and he's hooking us up."

Ted nodded, clearly hesitant to admit that Ford might not, in fact, be the enemy. He seemed like the kind of man who enjoyed a righteous fight, and he wasn't going to find one today. "That's great, honey, and, thank you." He gave Ford a grudging nod. "We've got plenty of talent and drive, all the plans worked out, but we're short on funding. The only way to bridge the gap between what we've got and what we need is to get the word out."

"Exactly. So, hopefully, you and I will go on the show, and after that, maybe things will start to come together more." Lily's voice soothed him, and Ford hoped that the television appearance would be the boon they hoped for.

"Well, thanks, then." Ford could tell that the concession wasn't easy for Ted.

"My pleasure, and really, if there's anything else you two can think of, I'm always glad to help."

After the visit, Ford lingered in the front hallway, giving Lily some privacy with her parents before they left. His phone buzzed in his pocket, but he ignored it. The hushed conversation in the kitchen was difficult to understand, but from what he gathered, they weren't thrilled with her decision to marry a Republican member of Congress. Between his parents and hers, with their divergent politics and wildly different family lives, he wondered if he'd made the right decision. Were they going to become a strong enough team to pull this off? Maybe their mutual attraction and easy chemistry wouldn't be enough to make it work, and for the first time since he'd decided to bring Lily into the campaign, he wondered if they were in over their heads.

She joined him, pulling the strap of her purse over her shoulder and looking exasperated. "Let's get out of here."

With an insistent tug on his sleeve, she dragged him out of the house, pulling the door closed behind them. The gorgeous sunny afternoon clashed with the tension they'd escaped. "Want to tell me what that was about?"

She blew out a breath, pushing her hair out of her face. "They can't resist putting their noses in my business, I guess." She urged him further down the sidewalk, toward the car. "I'm sorry. I really thought they would be so much more positive after all we've been through. Guess I was wrong."

He opened her door for her and waited until she dropped into the seat with a graceful swivel before closing the door and going around to the driver's side. "I couldn't hear what they were saying, but I could tell it was bad."

He started the car and turned the radio down, glancing over at her before checking his mirrors and pulling away from the Ashtons' house. "Did they try to talk you out of marrying me?"

"Not in so many words, but yes. They don't think we're a good fit, but it really doesn't matter. We don't have to be a good fit."

Her words hit him like a punch to the gut. Sure, logically he knew that their arrangement was not romantic and he shouldn't expect that she'd grow to love him or anything, but still. She must have been serious the other night when she stopped things from going too far between them. For her, their agreement was no more personal now than when they'd first made it.

He wanted their relationship to be more like what they were projecting, though, to do more. He checked his phone, glad to see the text he'd ignored was the news he was hoping for. "I have good news for you."

She turned to face him, the light catching subtle red highlights in her hair. "Oh yeah?"

"You and your dad are booked for *Good Morning, Dallas.* You've got the nine thirty slot after the cooking segment on Monday morning."

"Oh, Ford! Thank you so much." Lily unbuckled her seatbelt and pushed across the front seat to wrap him in a hug. "I really think it will do wonders for us."

The hug was awkward in the cramped space, but he didn't want her to let go and move back to her side. He kissed her temple, savoring the moment, glad that her parents' disapproval hadn't dampened her enthusiasm for him. Having secrets together and facing opposition made their bubble of privacy that much more intimate.

"It was no problem. I'd do that and more for you any day."

"Soldier On is so important to me, and it means a lot that you arranged this for us. I mean that."

She sat up, shifting in her seat as she buckled herself in. He watched her, glad to see her so happy. "If it's important to you, then it's important to me."

•••

The following morning, Lily left her apartment, running behind for a photo shoot. Somehow, the closer the location, the harder it was for her to leave on time. International flight and week-long assignment? No problem. Quick shoot at a local site? Not so much. She only had to drive to a nearby company headquarters for a shoot that would be used for internal communications, so her subconscious must have convinced her that she could sleep in. The fact that the company was a huge national corporation with thousands of employees who would see the materials did nothing to prompt her to get ready quickly.

After the disastrous visit with her parents, Ford had looked so deflated. But as far as she was concerned, she and Ford could declare their first victory, however small. The fact that she'd defended their engagement as though it were real gave her confidence that she could do it again if it came up. They knew her better than anyone, so if she could fool then, she could fool anyone. Her parents were ardently liberal, vehemently opposed to everything they thought Republicans stood for, so to have them accept Ford would be major. Too bad they'd shot that hope down before they even left. Not even waiting until they could speak privately, they'd voiced their concerns and objections, as nicely as they could, but strong and unmistakable nonetheless.

He'd hinted about his family life, and Lily had a good idea that it would be similarly difficult to sway his parents to their side. Having a win in their pockets would bolster her confidence, help her ignore the nagging thought that they'd made a huge mistake.

Distracted with thoughts of getting to work on time, her parents, and convincing everyone that their engagement was authentic, Lily didn't notice the people loitering in the common area outside her apartment building. When the first reporter approached her, she was caught completely by surprise.

"Good morning, Ms. Ashton, what can you tell us about your engagement to Congressman Richardson?" A young woman shoved a handheld recorder up to Lily's face and stayed with her, walking backwards as Lily tried to keep moving toward the parking lot.

"I don't know what you mean. There's nothing to tell," Lily answered, though she wasn't completely sure she should say anything. Perhaps "no comment" was more appropriate in these situations.

"What do you make of Sam Coldwell's accusations that your engagement is conveniently timed to coincide with next month's election?" The young woman continued, undaunted by Lily's short reply.

Lily stopped, frozen as the words hit her. "He said that?" Certain that she'd broadcast her guilt and confirmed what the reporter suspected, she consciously arranged her features in a way that she hoped was more neutral. Time for her years in front of cameras to pay off.

She'd tried to stay more informed about the congressional race now that she was a part of it, but she'd been preoccupied with work and Ford the last couple of days. In her rush to get ready and out the door that morning, she hadn't turned on the television or checked the news online. Never in her wildest dreams, or nightmares, would she have thought that anyone could guess what they were up to. They'd anticipated having to carefully convince people who knew them that they were sincere, but to have their true plan revealed so succinctly, and so quickly, was unnerving.

The reporter looked pleased that she'd caught Lily off guard and powered forward. "Yes, ma'am. He's questioning the authenticity of your relationship, asserting that your engagement is part of some elaborate scheme to win the election. Would you care to comment?"

"Um, no I wouldn't. No comment." Even if she had an appropriate response ready, Lily was certain that she'd give the truth away with her fumbling. Cursing her lack of preparation, she tried to edge past the reporter.

She stepped in front of Lily and continued to ask questions, remaining calm but firm. "What do you have to say about the fact that your engagement comes on the heels of Mr. Coldwell challenging Congressman Richardson's marital status?"

Brushing past the reporter and ignoring her shouted questions, Lily continued on toward the parking lot. She could easily answer with something about being a private person or wanting their relationship kept out of the public eye, but answering one question would lead to more. This could get out of hand very easily and quickly. She couldn't encourage it, couldn't take the chance.

The reporter and the cameraman with her trailed Lily, each question more provocative than the last, until she reached her car and slid inside. She watched the reporter tell the cameraman to stop filming, apparently admitting defeat at least for the time being. Surely this wasn't the last time these accusations would come up, and Lily wondered how long she could endure them before snapping. Hands shaking, she started her car and took a deep breath. She wanted to call Ford, to make some sense out of what had just happened, but she needed to leave. If she sat in the parked car too long, the team may decide it was worth another try and approach her again, either knocking on the window or blocking her way. She pulled out of the lot, concentrating on steadying her breath and paying attention to the road ahead.

• • •

After the photo shoot, during which she summoned every ounce of her professional reserve, Lily called Ford. The day of work dragged on, the hours ticking by at a glacial pace, with the morning's incident, the stress of keeping their secret, and the confusing emotions spiraling through her. Shoots always ran much longer than it seemed necessary, with every person involved having their own opinion about every minute detail of the campaign, but today was especially brutal.

"Hey, you." His voice came through the line, his baritone warm and welcoming. None of the panic or dread she'd been harboring all day was reflected in his tone. Despite the nerve-wracking day, a soothing calm washed over her at the rich sound of his voice. Whatever happened next, she wasn't facing it alone.

"Hey." She hesitated, wondering if he'd even heard about what was happening with the Coldwell campaign. "So, I had an interesting visitor this morning."

"Oh?" His voice held no hint of understanding. He still sounded playful and happy to hear from her. She hated to ruin his day, but there was no way around it and no more time to waste.

Why didn't he already know about this and have a plan to address it? It would've been so much easier if she wasn't the bearer of bad news. "A reporter came to my apartment building this morning and stopped me on the way to work." Saying it out loud made her realize that her privacy was likely a thing of the past now. "Fortunately, they didn't actually come knocking on my door, so I guess that's one good thing, but I'm sure it won't be long before that happens, too. She wanted to get a comment from me about the remarks your opponent has been making about our engagement."

"What remarks?" Tension crept into his voice.

"Apparently he's been saying that our engagement timing is a little too convenient to be believable, that it's all orchestrated for the campaign. Basically that he knows what we're up to." Why had she agreed to this? It was so obvious, and they hadn't even thought ahead enough to plan for when people connected the dots. What a mess.

He swore under his breath. "Okay, what did you say?"

She tried not to take offense at the thought that he even had to ask, but they were both in an unfamiliar situation. "I said no comment, and then I hurried to my car."

Her shocked reaction and fumbling reply likely signaled to the reporter that she was on the trail of a real story, but Lily kept that to herself. They probably had major damage control to do, and the details could wait. Ford and his campaign team came up with this brilliant engagement plan; now they could come up with a way to fix it.

"Good. That's good." She could almost hear the gears turning in his mind. Apparently, since she hadn't folded at the first sign of pressure, he was confident that they could prevail. "They'll twist anything you say, so never give them anything to use."

"So, you had no idea this was going on?" Wasn't he always connected to everything having to do with his campaign?

"None at all. I've been out of pocket all day, haven't even been to the office yet. I was meeting with a senior citizen advocacy group this morning, and the rest of the day was spent working with a group I need an endorsement from." When he paused, she could hear his car radio playing softly in the background. "I'm sure they've seen it at headquarters, though, and it's probably killing them that they haven't heard from me yet. Can you meet me at the campaign office? They wanted to meet you and brief you on upcoming events anyway."

"Sure, no problem." The last thing she wanted to do was meet with the team of advisors who'd dreamed up the genius scheme that got her into this mess, but they were in too deep now. As stressed as she was, it would be nice to share the burden if nothing else.

He gave her the address, and she navigated out of the parking lot, into the early evening traffic. Like it or not, some things had to be done.

• • •

Lily parked beside Ford's car in the parking lot and hurried toward the door before any more nosy reporters materialized. Was this to be her life until they either got married or ended things? Inside, the office was exactly like the campaign headquarters she'd seen in movies: abuzz with activity, machines whirring, phones ringing. It even smelled like coffee and warm copier paper. Sure, most movies didn't feature handsome congressmen striding across the room to greet their fiancées of convenience, but everything else was the same. He and his situation had created this problem for her, but watching him approach, handsome and confident, still made her stomach flip flop. Engagement of convenience or not, when they were in front of other people, they were on, so when he wrapped her in a quick hug and dropped a sweet kiss on her lips, she reciprocated.

"Thanks for getting here so quickly. The team has seen everything, and they're waiting for us in the conference room." His even tone and carefree smile belied the tension they both felt.

Ford took her hand and led her toward the conference room in the back of the building. The people at work in the office didn't try to hide their curiosity, openly staring at her and watching as they walked through the office. *Bad news travels fast.* She offered a bright smile to anyone who caught her eye, hoping to project a calm confidence. The mood in the conference room was decidedly less animated, and Lily's heart dropped when she saw the seven serious faces lining the table.

Taking her seat, she smiled and tried to appear comfortable as she faced the advisory team, who looked like they blamed her for the mess. Ford brought her a bottle of water and sat next to her. "Since we were both so busy today, we missed a lot, it seems. That reporter that visited you was only the tip of the iceberg."

Charlie welcomed her to the group and introduced her to the rest of the team. "We are so glad to have you on the team, Ms. Ashton. If you'll make sure Joelle has all your contact information, you can get all further communication electronically. For now, we have your information and schedule right here."

He passed a folder across the table to her, and she stopped herself from asking if it was a "Welcome to the Richardson Campaign" packet. "I'll do that; thank you."

As she flipped through the pages, she found advisory team member information, the basics of Ford's platform, a schedule of upcoming events, and a list of talking points. "Are these pre-written tweets?"

Robert cleared his throat. "Yes. Our social media intern prepared them. If you have an opportunity, we'd love for you to try to use any or all of them. It will be helpful in reaching the younger voters that we tend to lose to Democrats."

"I doubt that eighteen-year-olds are swayed by political tweets."

"It's just one of a many-pronged approach. It can't hurt." Robert shrugged. The reach for voters who traditionally identified as Democrats clearly wasn't a top priority. Lily assumed the Tea Party candidate was the real threat to Ford's re-election chances.

"Sure, I'm happy to help in any way that I can. And is it safe to assume that these are the events I'll need to attend?" She pointed out the highlighted entries on Ford's schedule.

"That's right. We would love to see you there, but so far none of them will require you to address the group or anything. That's really more for earlier in the election, so next time we might call on you." Next time? If everything went according to plan, she'd be Ford's *wife* the next time he ran for office. "And now, unfortunately, there is the unsavory business of our chief competitor's attack on your relationship." Charlie pulled out a tablet and brought up one example after another of Sam Coldwell sound bites, each one questioning their relationship or outright accusing the Richardson campaign of orchestrating the engagement to distract voters from the issues. Though it was true, Lily wondered what issues their engagement was distracting voters from. As far as she could tell, the only issue facing the campaign was created by Coldwell himself, who made Ford's bachelor status something to talk about.

"We haven't responded one way or another yet," Caroline said, interrupting her thoughts. "We have to do something, though; we can't simply allow this rhetoric to continue. Reacting too quickly has never been wise, so we're taking a moment to formulate our plan."

Ford leaned back in his chair, and Lily was amazed at how he could appear so unaffected in the face of this campaign crisis. He'd had more experience with the pressures of running for office, so maybe this wasn't the worst he'd experienced. "The way I see it, we either go on the offensive and push back, or we make a quick statement about the engagement and put more effort into showing our happy faces in public. I'm sure we could get a mushy statement about how very much in love we are, etcetera, etcetera, put together relatively quickly."

Hearing him address the matter so devoid of emotion made Lily glad she'd kept a bit of her desire to herself and never forgotten that this was all an elaborate agreement. In the cold light of the crisis, he didn't seem to mirror the complex development of emotions she'd struggled with. They had a good relationship, and they clearly liked each other, but the fact was that he needed this engagement. He wouldn't have proposed if his campaign hadn't depended on it. It was too easy to get caught up in the emotions their chemistry inspired, but they'd never agreed to anything more than an engagement. Not love. This was a strategy meeting, nothing more, and if she wanted to protect her heart she'd keep that in mind.

"The best bet is probably a combination of both—you know, hit it from every angle," Robert said, then paused to drain his takeout coffee cup and toss it into an overflowing garbage can full of similar cups. "You two will need to be seen together a lot while Ford's in town, both in candid situations and at planned events. Lily, if you could spare the time to accompany him to D.C., that would be even better. We'll put the word out and make sure that the press picks up on every appearance you make, even if it's nothing more than grabbing your morning coffee together or picking out your china pattern." He snapped his fingers. "Especially if it's picking out your china pattern. I'll bet we could get a wedding feature in *D Magazine* or *Texas Monthly*, and maybe one of those bridal magazines, and have them cover you planning the wedding. People eat that stuff up." She could practically see the gears turning in his mind as his plan took shape.

"Hey, that could work. I knew I hired you for a reason." Ford teased, drumming his fingers on the table as his mind went to work. Lily felt invisible, like the sliver of emotion that had cropped up between them was lost in the calculations happening in the conference room.

"That's why you pay me the big bucks." Robert sat back with a satisfied grin.

Lily had made no promises beyond the November election, but the engagement was starting to become more of a commitment than she'd agreed to. Ford had given her the impression that until Election Day, her only obligation was to keep up appearances. Now they had to start their bridal registry? Putting their wedding preparations in writing, and in magazines, and on television, documented for anyone interested in them, made everything much more difficult to back away from. How could she quietly end the engagement if that was her choice? She'd have to dismantle wedding registries, return early gifts, and broadcast the news that they'd broken up much wider than before. If they asked her to go ahead with wedding dress shopping, she'd have to put a stop to the runaway engagement train. If they had their way, she'd be chatting with a lifestyle reporter while she got her dress fitted. Her nonreturnable wedding dress.

"Excuse me, but would you prefer that I answer questions or not? The reporter this morning certainly had no trouble finding me, so there's no reason to think it won't happen again." Lily figured that if she was stuck following the team's approach, she might as well get with the program and put herself back in the discussion. Maybe they'd stop talking about her and her imaginary wedding like she wasn't in the room.

Caroline tapped her pen against the table, narrowing her eyes as she decided. "You know, I think we should address any further questions head on. Dodging the reporters makes it look like there's a story there, and we'd prefer that there's nothing for them to grab on to. You know what I mean? Keep it simple, though, and don't get caught explaining yourself or giving too many details. Something quick and breezy, like 'we're very happy together, thank you' should suffice."

"That's the truth," Ford added, lacing his fingers through hers and kissing her hand. "There's nothing more to the story than a simple engagement."

He wasn't even letting his team in on the discussions they'd had about his need for a fiancée. As far as they knew, she hadn't agreed to the engagement for his campaign; she'd said yes because they were in love.

Chapter Seven

Ford's parents loved throwing cocktail parties in their home: his father to socialize, network, and bring the kids together, his mother primarily to show off the family's art collection and excellent taste in expensive wine. When she entertained, she was in her element, buzzing through her home full of guests like the queen bee that she was. His engagement combined with the upcoming election was the perfect excuse for them to invite everyone who was anyone to celebrate, and their home was filled with laughter and animated conversation. Most men would probably introduce their fiancées to their parents during an intimate family dinner, but Ford knew better. After the awkward reception they'd received from Lily's parents, he was convinced that the more people around, the better. They'd do what they had to do, but the tension would be pleasantly diffused with the atmosphere and alcohol. Mother would certainly make her opinion, whatever it was, known, but at least with such a large audience, he wouldn't have to hear much about it tonight. The excellent wine and hors d'oeuvres were a bonus.

With a gentle hand on her arm above her elbow, Ford leaned down to whisper. "Nobody but Mother knows that the advisory team wanted me to get engaged. She may hint at it, but she won't tell my brothers or her friends."

"What about your dad?"

"I don't know if she's told him or not. He won't let it slip if she did, though. Just remember that as far as everyone else knows, this is a normal engagement."

"Got it." When she tilted her face toward him to answer, the light perfume she wore drifted up.

Ford's youngest brother, Grant, was in town from medical school for the party. He attended University of Texas in Austin, so he could make the quick trip home for the occasional family get-together as necessary. He was pouring a frothy beer from the keg behind the bar when he noticed Ford and waved them over.

"Hey!" Grant rounded the bar and pulled Ford into a bear hug, pounding him on the back a few times for good measure. "Dad said you were engaged, so I decided to finally come to one of these snoozefests and see for myself."

"I see. You'll make the drive to drink Dad's beer and meet a pretty girl, but not to help me get through any of the excruciating dinners they've been throwing for me lately." Ford kidded his brother and punched him on the shoulder.

"Hey, you know I'd love nothing more than to watch you talk about the same policies and political issues over and over again, but I kind of need to concentrate on school." Grant took a big drink of his beer.

"I guess I'll let you off the hook. I'd hate to be the reason you're not smart enough to avoid a malpractice suit someday."

Ford introduced Lily to his brother and enjoyed the way Grant's eyes widened in appreciation. Lily was stunning, and the more time he spent with her, the easier it was to forget what a shock it could be to meet her. His middle brother, Lincoln, was sipping his own beer and chatting with his long-time girlfriend across the room. Grant called to him over the humming conversation, apparently unfettered with the basic manners their mother had worked so hard to instill in them.

Grant and his girlfriend joined the group, and introductions were made. Ford took a moment to enjoy the ease with which Lily fit into the family. His brothers were easygoing and agreeable, but it couldn't be easy to meet everyone in the family all at once.

Lincoln's girlfriend, Serena, had finished her master's degree in social work earlier that year and had recently started a new job. "That's so cool that you'll have your own agency," she said to Lily. "The place where I work is having trouble paying the bills, and they are laying people off left and right. I work for a program that's funded by the government, so I'm not at quite as much at risk, but they pull those state dollars all the time apparently. I might come begging you for a job if they let me go."

"I'm sure we'd love to have you once we're up and running. We should get in touch when I actually know what kinds of positions we'll have available."

Serena and Lincoln had been together since college, so she might as well be a part of the family. She was the daughter of one of Mother's best friends and definitely didn't need to worry about money if she got laid off. It was nice to see the women in their lives networking and getting along so easily, though.

"So, Lily, have you met the parents yet?" Mischief sparkled in Grant's eyes.

"Not yet. Any tips?" Lily looked like she knew there was a joke she wasn't quite in on.

"Wear a jacket." Serena took an innocent sip from her straw and fluttered her eyelids at Lincoln. "What? Your mother can be a bit chilly."

Lincoln put his arm around her shoulders and kissed her temple. To Lily, he tried to be reassuring. "You have to meet her, but you don't have to prolong it. Get in, get out, and save yourself."

Serena added, "I wish I could say he was kidding."

The group laughed, but nobody was really joking. It wasn't going to be an easy, warm reception and Ford knew it. The sooner he introduced Lily to his parents, the sooner it would be over. His father was entertaining a small group of friends, so Ford excused himself and Lily to join them. Holding hands, they casually joined the intimate circle. After the group's laughter at Dad's joke died down, Ford made use of the opening.

"Dad, I'd like you to meet Lily Ashton, my fiancée." Ford held his breath as he scanned the room, looking for Mother. His father would love anyone he brought home, would be charming and agreeable no matter what he actually thought of her, and Ford didn't worry for a second that Lily would feel right at home. Growing up with Buck Richardson as his example was where Ford learned how to charm people no matter the situation, to bring them to his way of thinking. It had been perhaps his most powerful asset in his campaign. Buck never met a stranger, and he had a way of loosening purse strings when it came to campaigns he cared about. His mother, on the other hand, had laid the sweetness in her voice on a little too thick to be believable when they spoke on the phone earlier, so he knew he was in for a tough time.

His father shook Lily's hand, beaming down at her warmly. "We've heard so much about you. It's nice to meet you, dear." He was practiced at making people comfortable, and he put his charms to work on Lily right away. "I'm only sorry that Ford took so long to bring you home. Where has he been hiding you?"

Lily was clearly flattered by his attention. "Thank you for having me, Mr. Richardson. You have a gorgeous home." A bit of tension left Ford's shoulders. Lily was a natural in social settings and could hold her own; he shouldn't have worried. Between his father's practiced social graces and Lily's natural charisma, he could likely leave them alone and confront his mother head on.

"Call me Buck, honey. You're family now. Where are my manners? Let's get you a drink." His father flagged down a passing waiter and pulled two glasses of red wine from the tray and handed one to Lily. "I hope you like red, because this is one of my favorites. Jessica and I discovered this fantastic winery in Napa on vacation last year. Ever since our trip, we've been sure to always have it on hand. Now, I'd like to propose a toast." Ford took another glass from the tray and raised it in anticipation as several guests joined the loosely formed circle.

"Thank you to everyone, our dearest friends and colleagues, who came to celebrate tonight. We are so proud of Ford and all he's accomplished, and now we're thrilled to add his beautiful fiancée to the family." Dad raised his glass and smiled at Lily, sincere welcome in his eyes. "To Ford and Lily, a beautiful couple with a bright future. I look forward to dancing at your wedding." Everyone tipped their glasses and drank to them, murmuring their well wishes. Ford accepted the group's congratulations but kept an eye out for his mother.

Her entrance was timed perfectly to ensure maximum impact. She sauntered toward them in a cloud of condescension and expensive perfume, her eyes focused on the trio. "Buck, why didn't you tell me our guest of honor was here?" She turned and swiped a glass from the waiter's tray. "You must be Lily. Welcome to our home; I'm Jessica Richardson. It's a pleasure to meet you." His brother was right; Lily should've worn a jacket.

Lily shook Mother's hand and looked her in the eye with a confidence he rarely saw in the women he introduced to his family. Either she didn't realize who she was dealing with or didn't care, because she didn't shrink away or flinch from the acid cloaked in sugar in Mother's tone. Whichever it was, standing beside a woman who didn't wither under Mother's gaze was a novel experience, one Ford hadn't realized he'd enjoy quite so much.

"Mrs. Richardson, it's so nice to finally meet you." Lily's smile appeared to be genuine, likely the result of many years' worth of practice. Being a professional model was coming in handy. He waited for Mother to insist that Lily call her Jessica, or at least pretend she accepted that Lily was joining the family.

"I'm afraid Rutherford hasn't told us much about you, but you look awfully familiar. What is it that you do?" Jessica Richardson sipped her wine, never breaking eye contact with Lily as she waited for the answer.

Of course Mother knew Lily was a model. She was likely asking so she could gauge Lily's reaction as she looked down her nose at her, to see how easy it was to shrink her with a single look. Mother never said anything by accident.

Lily took a sip from her glass. "I'm a model. You've probably seen one of my ads or something." Ford silently dared Lily to talk about Soldier On, to watch Mother try not to choke on her drink at the thought of a liberal marrying into the family, but no such luck. Serena got a pass from Mother because of her family. As long as she came from good stock, her job was irrelevant.

Mother looked decidedly disappointed when Lily neither withered under her gaze nor looked apologetic about her profession. "Perhaps that's it, but you do seem awfully familiar."

Mother drained her glass and set it on a table, likely certain that it would be collected by the catering staff before anyone noticed it was there. "Perhaps you have a familiar face, then. You kids enjoy the party. Be sure to try the shrimp tartlets; I hear they are positively divine." She waved to a woman Ford recognized from the garden club, the diamonds in her tennis bracelet catching the light with every movement. Before he had a chance to register relief that the encounter had been so quick and painless, Mother laid her hand on his forearm. "Ford, dear, don't leave before I give you the check the Carmichaels sent over for your campaign."

"I've got it in the study, actually," Ford's father chimed in. "They send their regrets for missing the party tonight. Let me go ahead and give it to you now so we don't forget."

With his hand engulfing hers, Ford led Lily through the crowded great room toward the hallway leading to his father's study. He watched her eyes flick across the family's home, appraising the sumptuous furnishings and artwork. As well-traveled as she was, Lily had an eye for good art and would probably enjoy lingering at some of the family's nicer pieces.

"Lily, if you'd like to wait out here for a moment and check out the art, my parents have some incredible pieces. I won't be long." Glad to give her something to do besides worry about scrutiny from his mother, he showed her to the first piece.

She needed no further encouragement and stopped in front of a Rembrandt etching his family had purchased when they first began collecting art for the home. Ford followed his father into the study, intending to collect the check and spend the rest of the evening entertaining Lily.

•••

Lily suppressed the urge to run her fingertips over the priceless art lining the home's hallway. Footsteps rounded the corner, and she smiled, ready to make conversation with Ford's mother. The greeting died on her lips when Jessica Richardson flicked a look of icy disdain in Lily's direction and brushed past her, disappearing into the study and closing the door behind her. Soft light and movement filtered through the door's hammered glass insert. Though she wasn't usually an eavesdropper, Lily found herself edging closer to the study, quietly listening for a clue about what was happening on the other side.

"Really, Rutherford, a model? Why didn't you just find a nice Hooters girl to bring home? Don't you think you're taking the trophy wife to a new extreme?" Jessica's voice carried past the closed door, as though she didn't care if she was overheard or not.

"Mother, what are you talking about? I told you at lunch that Lily is a model." His voice was calm, but there was an edge of impatience.

"Honestly, I can't believe you're actually going through with this. Are you trying to humiliate me or commit career suicide?"

"I think that's a bit extreme." Lily could picture Ford's jaw clenching as he kept his voice calm. "You're overreacting."

"Of all the potential wives available to you, did you even once consider one of the nice girls from Junior League? Did you look at the women your team went to the trouble to find for you? Ones who were appropriate? It would've been nice if you'd chosen someone with a more substantial background, or at least someone more educated."

"Jessica, come on now." Buck interrupted, though his tone said he knew his words would fall on deaf ears. "We trust that the team knows what they're doing when they say Ford needs to get married. It's lucky that he was already seeing someone that he has feelings for. It shouldn't matter if she's from a certain family or doesn't have an education."

"Lily is a college graduate, Mother, and while I don't think she's in Junior League, she's certainly civic-minded. I don't have to defend her or my decisions to you, but she is definitely a woman of substance. Not that this is any of your business."

The pause that followed was likely accompanied by a look that would turn a lesser man to stone. As horrifying as it was to be torn to shreds by his mother, being defended by Ford was gratifying. They'd been put through their paces with the engagement going public, and at every obstacle, he'd been there ready to fight for her, more than she ever would have expected. "If you intend on bringing someone into this family, it's most certainly my business. We're talking about our family, Ford. You are much too cavalier if you think any woman off the street is appropriate to bring into this home without a thought to how it affects everyone else."

Ford's words were soft, and Lily had to lean so close to the door in order to hear that if someone opened it, they'd hit her head. "We will not do this, Mother. With or without your approval, this engagement is going forward. Lily will be a Richardson, and it is your choice whether you embrace that reality or not. Whatever you decide, though, listen closely, because I'm only going to say it once. Regardless of your opinion, you will respect her, or you will not see me or any grandchildren until you do. I'm quite serious, and I won't listen to you talk about her like this again. Am I making myself clear?"

Jessica sputtered, but acquiesced. "Of course, Rutherford. I wouldn't dream of interfering with your marriage." The prospect of losing contact with her son and potential grandchildren must have hit home. A woman like Jessica likely prided herself on being the center of a strong family, and she couldn't allow a rift of that size to develop. Lily could picture Jessica holding her head high, swallowing her pride like a bitter pill with every word she bit out.

Grandchildren? Their fake engagement suddenly became much more real. Either Ford was an excellent actor, or he was more invested in their relationship than she realized. Either way, it was hot, and the shiver that skipped down her spine was unmistakable.

His father cleared his throat behind the door. "So, how about I get you that check?"

Terrified she'd be caught eavesdropping, Lily rushed to the far end of the hall, reaching a marble statue in time to arrange her features in casual appreciation before Ford pushed the door open and stormed out. Intensity burned in his eyes as he barreled toward her, rendering her speechless and powerless over her limbs. The strength she'd heard in his voice behind the door was evident in every motion he made, in the way he breathed, turning her knees to jelly.

With a firm but gentle hand on her arm, he pulled her the few steps down the hall into a luxuriously appointed library. Bookcases lined the walls, stretching from floor to ceiling, and plush carpeting muffled every sound except Ford's breathing. Silently, purposefully, he closed the door behind them and engaged the lock.

Lily opened her mouth to speak, to slice through the tension that twanged between them like piano wire. Ford closed the distance between them, his mouth sweeping over hers before a thought could form. Her arms encircled his warm, strong torso as he backed her up against a bookcase full of beautiful leather bound classics. A thick tome toppled off, bouncing softly against the carpet, and he pushed it aside with his foot. Sure, unwavering fingertips skimmed her ribcage through the satiny fabric of her dress, and every hesitation melted away with the warmth of his body pressed against hers. Raking her fingers through his thick hair, she opened her mouth to accept him as he deepened the kiss. Time stopped, everything disappearing but the sound of her heartbeat thundering in her ears, when Ford cupped her jaw in his hands. Gone was the casual attraction, the occasional indulgence in their chemistry. In its place was desire, a passion demanding acknowledgement.

Meeting his gaze was almost too intense, too real, to face, but Lily couldn't look away as he pulled back and looked into her eyes. Everything around them faded away, until it was only the two of them in the world and nothing else mattered. Ford was all she could see. Emotions she hadn't experienced or seen reflected in a man's eyes in years played across his features, giving form to the intense attachment she hadn't been able to admit to herself.

"I never thought I would fall for anyone again, never wanted to. I thought you were a safe bet, that we could keep things from going too far." His lips brushed against hers, softly sending sparks of pleasure through her, before he continued. "I was wrong."

"I felt the same way, but now I'm not so sure." She couldn't believe she was admitting to going beyond the superficial, actually giving voice to thoughts she'd kept carefully hidden.

"This is real." His voice was little more than a whisper, but there was no hesitation. "You and me. We don't have to pretend it isn't. We shouldn't lie to ourselves anymore."

Tears welled in her eyes, threatening to spill over, and a lump formed in her throat as she nodded. "I know. You're right." Her answering whisper was rough with both the beauty and the heartache of the moment. So many years had been dedicated to guarding her heart, keeping her love for her husband locked inside. Letting Ford in was a defeat as much as it was a joy, but he was right. It was real. And she didn't want to hide from love any longer.

With every obstacle they faced, every person they encountered who questioned their relationship, the fledgling feelings between them grew. Shoring up their resolve to present a united front had forced them into a bubble of intimacy, of a shared goal, and every challenge brought them closer. She was tired of holding back, done telling herself she couldn't fall for him.

"I could fall in love with you, Lily," Ford whispered before capturing her lips in a kiss. She couldn't answer him, couldn't bring herself to admit that much out loud, but she knew it was true for her as well. Ford was proving to be exactly the man she'd dreamed of, the man she secretly hoped he would be.

As he urged her lips opened and deepened the kiss, his mouth tasting of the wine they'd had earlier, she surrendered. The longing she'd suppressed unfurled along with the desire she'd denied. Freed from the self-imposed constraints, she answered his kiss with an urgency that grew with every moment. As though sensing the change in her, his movements became more purposeful, his kiss infused with passion they couldn't express with words, his hands exploring her body with a new sense of freedom.

His mouth burned a hot trail across her chest as he dipped his head to capture the soft tops of her breasts exposed by her dress's low neckline. The groan that rumbled deep in his throat hummed across her skin while he worked one hand beneath the hem of her dress and kept the other steady with a firm hold around her back. Finding her ready and willing, with none of her past hesitance, he worked his fingers beneath the thin fabric of her panties. For a moment, everything around them fell away, and the only sound was their breath in the hushed room. Ford's blue eyes pierced the haze of need, of want, between them and asked without a word if she wanted the same thing. To answer his silent question, she nodded and moved to unbuckle his pants. He sucked in a sharp breath, encouraging her as she pushed his clothes down his thighs and slipped out of her panties. Glad she'd planned ahead, she fumbled with the clasp on her handbag and fished out a condom. With a wicked grin, Ford took it while she tossed her bag to the floor.

For a second, his eyes bounced around the room. Settling on the leather chaise situated in the corner, he picked her up until her legs wrapped around his torso and carried her the short distance. A throaty laugh escaped her as the carefree joy of being carried washed over her. Ford buried his face in the soft spot where her neck met her shoulders and kissed her as he set her down. The soft leather was cool to the touch as he stretched out over her. In the soft light of the Tiffany-style floor lamp he ran his fingers through her hair, slowing the manic pace. In his eyes, a new depth of understanding grew, a sense of surrender she'd never seen before. At once, the change between them was forever in the making and completely unexpected.

When he lowered himself, she tightened her arms around his shoulders, pulling him closer for a searing kiss. Reveling in the moment, she explored every inch of Ford she could get her hands on. Starting with his thick, silky hair, she worked her way down, across the soft planes of his muscled shoulders, down to his waist, where she skimmed his ribcage with her fingertips. He sucked in a breath as her hands dipped further, finally discovering the unmistakable evidence that he wanted her.

Encouraged, he rocked back on his heels until he could free both hands to do his own exploring. He covered the curves of her body with his feather-soft touch until she couldn't wait any longer. Pulling him down to her, she guided his hands under her dress to show him how ready she was. His eyes blazed with intensity, and without further hesitation, he entered her in one smooth, certain motion. With a sharp gasp, her eyes flew wide open and then squeezed shut as she gave in to the delicious moment. Magic stretched out between them, sweet and shimmery for a few perfect seconds. It was perfect, and worth the wait.

Their mouths locked, the kiss as mesmerizing as the steady movement of Ford's sure strokes. Head buzzing, lost in the sensations flooding her body, her climax began to build, rolling through her body. Both unsure she could handle any more and not wanting it to end, she pushed against Ford and tightened her grip on him when he answered with a matched intensity. With a cry that was muffled against Ford's neck, she released the last bit of tenuous control and gave in. Moments later, Ford followed and gently rolled to her side to nestle against her.

Breath slowing but still heavy, he braced himself against the arm of the chaise and kissed her. A perfect, solid kiss that said everything they never had. Without words, she knew they were thinking the same thing, that something had shifted between them, that the old worries and hurts didn't matter when it came to what they shared. That they were together now, and it was real. Though she'd fought against it for so long, had never seriously considered the possibility of falling for anyone else, the panic she expected wasn't there, just the blissful peace of giving in to what her heart truly wanted.

They stayed fitted together on the chaise, sleepy and sated. Lily's eyes wandered across the bookshelf closest to them, and she slowly noticed the titles.

"Who's the Danielle Steel fan?" What had to be a complete collection of the author's work lined the shelves in alphabetical order. "And Nora Roberts?" A similarly full collection was housed above the Steel books.

Ford's laugh rumbled deep in his chest. "Mother. She's a voracious reader."

"I would've expected something a little more, I don't know, cold. Her taste in fiction makes me like her a little more." The more titles she noticed, ranging from historical romances to popular women's fiction, the funnier it became. If pressed, she would have guessed that Jessica Richardson spent any free time she had perfecting her resting bitch face. Finding out she had a secret life as an actual human being was a refreshing surprise.

"Don't let her book collection sway you. She's just as bad as you thought. In fact, I don't think there's any reason for us to stick around and see her again tonight. What do you say we get out of here and go home?" Ford let his hand slip over her hip and rest on her butt, giving her a little squeeze.

"That sounds perfect." With a lazy smile, Lily stretched on the chaise. Disentangling themselves from the cozy cocoon was the last thing she wanted to do, but leaving the party promised privacy. "I think I'd like to see what you can accomplish in an actual bed." She waggled her eyebrows comically, but they both knew she wasn't joking.

Sufficiently motivated, they got dressed, smoothing their clothes and hair so they'd appear normal when they returned to the party. Ford carefully returned the books that had been pushed around on the shelves to their previous perfection, then took her hand and pulled her closer to press a kiss to her lips.

"We'll slip out. I can't think of anyone out there I'd like to spend time with when I could have you all to myself." He unlocked the door. "I don't know about you, but that was over much too quickly for me."

They rushed through the empty hallway, suppressing laughs, and left his parents' house through a side door, completely unnoticed.

• • •

Lily and her father had their big interview on *Good Morning, Dallas* early the next morning, so she had to leave Ford hours before she was finished exploring the new development in their relationship. Leaving Ford's bed was torture after spending a few blissful hours letting him demonstrate just how much more time he wanted to spend pleasing her. She definitely looked forward to seeing what else he had in store for her. The newfound perfection in their match intoxicated her, changing the dynamic she'd worked so hard to preserve and making her crave his embrace as soon as she left. Having everything she'd believed for so long shattered so completely made her wonder why she'd ever fought her feelings in the first place.

She locked up behind her and toed her shoes off near the front door. Sinking her feet into the plush carpet, Lily paused for a moment. Was this really happening? Was it time to move on? Everything about her marriage to Nathan was unique to that relationship, but at the core, the elements that she'd loved the most were growing between her and Ford now. She considered the evening they'd shared and her realizations about him as she got ready for bed. Finding a man who was interesting and made her feel beautiful was easy. Finding one whom she could respect, who would protect her, whose confidence in their relationship was unshakeable, well, that was rare. Being forced into the bubble of secrecy surrounding the circumstances of their engagement had done nothing but bring them closer. Intimacy that could have otherwise taken years to develop, if it ever did, seemed to have blossomed with every interaction.

Lily was about to crawl into bed when her eyes fell on a framed picture of Nathan on her nightstand. She saw the picture every day, and her reaction to it depended on how life was going at the time. Sometimes seeing his face made her smile at the memories she'd kept so close, sometimes anger at being left to pick up the pieces surprised her, and sometimes she was simply sad. Over the years, the soul-buckling pain of the tragic loss had gradually smoothed out into a bittersweet melancholy. She missed him, thought of him every day, and wished more than anything that he hadn't been taken from her so quickly, but she accepted her reality. A big part of that was her unwillingness to move on, and she knew that. As long as she told herself that nobody could replace Nathan, she never had to truly give him up.

It was time.

Instead of going to bed, Lily pulled Nathan's footlocker out of her closet and popped the lid open. When the tears she'd expected didn't surface, she knew she was right. It was past time to put her marriage to bed and move forward. With a tender fondness, she retrieved her photos, wedding mementos, and the stuffed tiger dressed in a camouflage uniform Nathan had left in his place when he deployed. He'd given it to her in a lighthearted moment before he left, trying to tackle the serious matter of his mortality, reminding her to be brave and unafraid of what could lie ahead. Neither of them believed she'd be put to the test so quickly. With every item she tucked into the footlocker, her heart lightened. She ran her hands lightly over his things, remembering the feel of his strong body when they hugged, and felt comforted instead of heartbroken. His handwriting peeked out beneath a picture, reminding her of the intense, all-consuming love they'd shared, and her heart didn't clutch, just kept beating normally. Everything was going to be okay.

With a whispered "goodbye for now," she closed the lid and sat on the foot of her bed. Ford wouldn't replace Nathan. Nobody could ever do that, but finally, after years of holding on, she was ready to let go. The engagement that began as a favor was now as real as they'd been pretending, and she looked forward to opening up her life and heart to a new love. A perfect calm fell over her with the realization, and she knew Nathan would want a happy future and another love for her.

Chapter Eight

Still humming from the amazing turn of events, Ford couldn't stop smiling. Never in a million years would he have guessed that his mother's disapproval would provide the impetus for the change between him and Lily. It was amazing, perfect even, to simply open himself up to the possibility that he'd fall in love again. No more pretending he didn't want it, no more guarding his heart and reactions, making sure he never cared more than Lily. This could really work. Maybe their engagement could turn into something real. He watched as Lily and Ted prepared for their interview on *Good Morning, Dallas*.

"Are you nervous?" Lily caught her father's eye in the mirror as they sat in hair and makeup. They looked so much alike that Ford felt himself softening toward Ted. Who knew he was such a romantic?

"Not about the interview, but maybe a little about the makeup. What will your mother think?" He laughed as Lily's favorite makeup artist tucked tissue paper under his collar and swirled a fluffy brush in makeup. He made faces in the mirror as she went to work, then balled up the tissue and tossed it in a nearby wastebasket when she finished. "I have time for a quick trip to the men's room, right?"

"Sure. There's a cooking segment before us, then the commercial break." She watched her father disappear down the hallway and turned to Ford. "I can't believe how quickly you were able to get us this interview." She reached out and took the hand he stretched toward her from the next chair, pulling him closer for a quick kiss. "Thank you."

"It was no problem, and absolutely my pleasure. I hope the donations start rolling in as soon as people hear your story." After last night, he'd do anything to make her happy.

"And, speaking of pleasure, last night was really something, huh?" She dropped her eyes and tugged gently on his tie, urging him closer to her.

Bracing himself on the arms of her chair, he leaned in for a proper kiss. Careful not to muss her hair, he breathed her in. The clean, enchanting scent of her, soap, shampoo, and Lily herself, spun around him, drawing him closer. He nipped her earlobe and whispered, "Best. Night. Ever."

Goosebumps erupted on her forearms, and she shivered at his words, delighting him and making him wish they were anywhere but on the set of a local morning talk show. Ted rounded the corner, and Ford straightened, clearing his throat and stepping back a bit.

"Looks like you're just in time. They're giving you the signal." Ford checked his phone before silencing the ringer and standing. "You two have fun out there. I'll be watching from here, cheering you on."

Lily stood and joined her father, throwing Ford a dazzling smile as the production staff buzzed around them, attaching their wireless microphones and battery packs, checking levels, and directing them to their spots on the set. They greeted the show's host, Kelly Kiernan, and took their seats on the guest couch. Ted shifted, tugged on his collar, and nearly unplugged his microphone. Lily whispered something to him, and he laughed, visibly relaxing. She was a natural, so comfortable in front of the camera that she may as well be in the host's living room. That easy charisma would go far during the interview. Viewers would get a sense of how passionate Lily was about the issues and, with any luck, be persuaded to answer their call to action. The show came back from the commercial break, and the cameraman gave Kelly the signal.

"Good morning, Dallas! Thank you for joining us," Kelly said with a television-ready smile before sipping from her coffee mug.

"Today our guest is someone you've probably seen before, Lily Ashton. You might recognize Lily from the gorgeous Neiman Marcus billboard on Central Expressway. If you haven't seen that, you may have seen her online or in the paper with her handsome fiancé, Congressman Ford Richardson. He's running for re-election, so do check our website for information on how and where to vote in November." She set her coffee mug on the table in front of them and continued. "Our segment isn't about the upcoming election, though. Lily joins us today with her father, Ted Ashton, to talk about something a bit more serious than fashion and weddings. They're creating a new nonprofit organization, and I can't wait to hear all about it." She nodded toward each of them. "Welcome."

"Thank you for having us, Kelly," Ted answered.

Ford took a sip of coffee and rocked back on his heels as he watched the interview. Lily was a natural, both competent and relatable, but Ted was the one who surprised him. From their limited interactions, it seemed like he was passionate about issues, but not incredibly knowledgeable about how to address them without becoming confrontational. When they'd met in her parents' home, Ted seemed too emotional to separate himself from the issue enough to appear credible. Today he was on-point and relatable, appearing to be an expert on the subject. The duo came across as passionate but smart, and viewers were likely being rallied to the cause as they went on. Ford listened as Ted and Lily described the troubles facing military widows and widowers returning to civilian life as well as the concrete steps their organization would take to help them. As far as he could tell, the interview was a slam dunk.

"Lily, would you say that your experience with being a young military widow was the impetus for this project?" Kelly leaned forward as she asked, her eyes conveying the perfect blend of sympathy and interest.

Lily shifted on the couch, and her father patted her shoulder. "Of course that was a big part of it, Kelly. I doubt I'd know much about this issue without having had that experience. I was lucky, though, and I came home to a loving family, supportive friends, and the chance to start a new career, so I didn't face most of the issues we're concerned with. Not everyone has the same advantages. Unfortunately, it was easier for me to become successful because I was still so young when my husband died, and I hadn't become entrenched in the army life yet."

"There was still a chance for her," Ted added. "She was young enough that opportunities were still available to her."

The host's brow furrowed. "So, are you saying that if Lily's husband had not been killed so soon after they married, if he'd had a long military career before passing away, then her situation could've been worse?"

Ted cleared his throat, seeming to struggle with his answer before sitting up straighter. Ford could practically see the moment when Ted's mood switched from calm and competent to angry about the situation. "Yes, Kelly, I think I would say that. The women we've been working with are often completely lost when they come to us, and I know there are many more men and women out there just like them. There is such a need for these services that we simply cannot continue to work piecemeal. Sure, we can address a need here and there with our resources, but we need a more complete approach. We're starting Soldier On because these people need and deserve a place where they can start over."

"They're completely lost, Ted? Does the military not provide for their needs?" Kelly pushed further, and Ford wondered if she was more interested in a salacious segment than the simple informational spot they'd originally agreed upon.

"Sure, Kelly, it's not as though these spouses are kicked off post as soon as word comes in that their husbands or wives have passed away," Lily chimed in, smoothing out the situation with a calm explanation of the military wife's perspective. "But you have to understand that the life of a military spouse, especially a wife, can be all-consuming. Imagine following your husband around the world, from post to post, moving whenever he gets his orders. Maybe you keep in touch with friends and family, maybe you don't. You may not stay in the same place long enough to create lasting relationships, and when you do, inevitably you or your friends move on."

"I see. Having a strong support system in place is invaluable for anyone, though. What makes the situation unique for the people you want to serve?" Kelly continued, and Ford wasn't sure he liked the direction things were headed. Ted was becoming louder and more agitated with each question he answered. If Kelly let him get going, they could have a disaster on their hands.

"Kelly, we're meeting women all the time who need housing and health care. They need education or job training, something to help them get on their feet and learn how to support themselves and their children for the long term. Many widows are able to move on, but just as many spent their time in the military supporting their husbands' careers, and they were proud to do it." Lily paused and swallowed. "We as a society celebrate that devotion to service, and we expect nothing less. But what happens when there's no husband left to support? It's so easy to look the other way, or to assume that the army will care for these families."

Ted jumped in. "And we have no reason to believe that it will. Just look around at the soldiers who did make it home but are unemployed, unable to get necessary medical care, or are suffering from PTSD. Where's the army? Where's the government?"

Kelly looked thoughtful. "Do you think the shortcomings in the treatment of discharged veterans correlates to what happens to widows and widowers?"

"Absolutely!" Ted was on a roll, his voice raised to a near-shout. "I recently read that twenty-two veterans commit suicide every day. Twenty-two! That's more than we lose in combat! And it's unacceptable."

"I'm not sure about those numbers, but I do agree that there are some troubling issues facing our military and veterans."

"Troubling issues? Try a national travesty. It's disgraceful, and I've had it with the idiots in Washington who make decisions from the safety and comfort of their overpriced offices that affect real people's lives."

Ford's phone buzzed in his pocket. The interview was live, and his team was likely watching. With the negative turn the conversation had taken, he knew better than to slip out of the studio and answer. There was nothing he could do about it now, and if they were going to spin it, the team was probably already on the case. Kelly Kiernan continued with the segment, and Ted's answers became increasingly critical of the military, the current administration, and politicians in general, though Lily remained calm, continually trying to gently return the conversation to Soldier On. There was nothing he could do to stop the runaway train of blame and vitriol.

To Ford's relief, Lily finally patted her father's hand and interjected, putting an end to the diatribe. "Before we get any more off topic, I'd like to simply say that the sole purpose of Soldier On always has been and always will be to empower women. That's our mission at its core, and that doesn't change with politics or personal beliefs. Our services are available to women anywhere on the spectrum of need, from those who need no more than a couple of referrals to those who need to completely start over. We have no political agenda or affiliation, we're interested in serving those who served our country, and we must have community support in order to do so."

Kelly smiled at Lily's attempt to rein her father in and followed her lead, wrapping up the interview on a positive note. Ford breathed a sigh of relief, knowing that Ted had caused some serious damage, but at least it was over. "Sounds like Soldier On will be a tremendous asset to the community. What can people do to get involved?"

Lily thanked Kelly for not further agitating her father with a grateful expression before she answered. "More than anything, we need money and manpower. We've secured our basic funding, but realistically we need long-term corporate partnerships and the support of generous private donors to fully realize our mission. Our goal is to become a one-stop shop for services, so we have need for supplies, volunteers, and donations. We have opportunities to get involved at every level, and we welcome help however it comes, so please don't shy away if you're an individual." Her winsome smile betrayed the dismay she must be feeling, and Ford worried about how let down she would be now that their big chance at publicity had taken the sour turn.

His phone buzzed again, and he turned it off. The damage was done, and there was nothing left to do but to wait and see how bad the fallout would be.

Chapter Nine

A few hours later, Ford took his seat at the conference table and gratefully accepted the coffee Joelle set in front of him, thinking they were probably settling in for a long meeting. The serious faces of his advisors made him wish he'd stayed in the parking lot, but it was time to assess the damage Lily's appearance on *Good Morning, Dallas*, if any, had done to his campaign. He couldn't expect to control or spin everything she said, but it would have been nice if the public had a bit longer to get to know them as a couple before anything controversial popped up. Between this and the Coldwell campaign's assault on their engagement, damage control was becoming more daunting. Whatever the result, he had to get to work on repairing the public's perception. With any luck, the interview was no more than a blip on the radar and he could move on without worry.

"So, it's safe to assume that you all saw Lily's interview and that's why you called this emergency meeting?" Ford met the seven pairs of eyes watching him around the table and took a sip of coffee.

Charlie Tibbals cleared his throat, looking uncomfortable. "Ford, I'll level with you. It's not good."

Ford's heart sank. Even when things with the campaign were bleak, Charlie generally tried to remain optimistic. This was not a good sign. "All right, how bad is it? Give it to me."

Caroline spoke up. "Photos of your fiancée at her late husband's funeral have been everywhere. I'm not sure how you missed it, in fact." She turned her laptop so the screen faced him and clicked through several websites.

He'd missed it because he knew his team wouldn't, so why go looking? Why search for trouble when it was waiting for him at the office? Bad press popped up whenever anything even remotely related to his campaign happened, so the feeding frenzy must be in full force after the interview. The shift in his relationship with Lily was still so new; it seemed too fragile to expose to an assault like this, so he'd ignored it as long as he could. Unfortunately, his campaign couldn't hit pause while he enjoyed the bloom of new love, so his team powered through.

Each article or political forum Caroline clicked on her screen showed the same picture of Lily seated in the front row of a group of mourners, in between her parents. The closed coffin, covered in flowers, sat a mere yard away from her. A uniformed officer knelt before her, presenting a folded United States flag, his eyes full of sympathy and gratitude. Lily's hands covered the lower half of her face, her expression one of fathomless grief. He remembered seeing the picture in the local paper. Though he and Lily rarely spoke of her husband beyond facts and the occasional memory, the powerful image of his fiancée mourning her husband told him all he needed to know about her first marriage.

"I know it's a surprise to some people that Lily was married before, and the fact that she's the widow of a soldier adds to that, but is it really that bad?" They wouldn't be so worried if it wasn't, but Ford couldn't shake the idea that they could overcome a little hitch in the plan.

Caroline pushed printouts toward him. "Here. It's not just that Lily was married, nor that she's a widow. It's the connection bloggers and dozens of people on social media are making, that Lily is anti-war and therefore anti-military, after losing her husband."

"That's preposterous." Ford skimmed the articles they'd printed out for him, including several Tea Party blogs, some ultra-conservative organizations' Facebook pages, and commenters on the news stories. It was ridiculous, but Caroline was right. People had taken the assumption and run with it, each comment or assumption more outrageous than the last. More than a few had questioned his patriotism and support of the military because of his relationship with Lily. "How did this get so far out of hand?"

"It's election season in Texas. The crazier, the better," Robert answered. "You know Coldwell is eating this up. At this point, he doesn't even have to fan the flames. He can just sit back and watch."

"Exactly," Caroline added. "Every crackpot blogger is taking the story and blowing it up. Some of them are actually persuasive, making the case for Lily's anti-military leanings based on both the loss of her husband and the fact that we haven't been talking about him."

"What we can't figure out is how you decided that keeping her past a secret from us was a good idea. We can't advise you if we don't have the whole story. You know that." Charlie's mouth set in a grim line, his eyes reflected the defeat the entire team apparently felt.

"I wasn't keeping anything a secret." Ford knew it wasn't entirely true, but he'd never lied to them or avoided answering questions about Lily. They didn't ask if she'd been married before, and he didn't tell them. "As soon as I did what you wanted and got engaged, you all checked that off your list and moved on. I would've told you anything you wanted to know about Lily. All you asked was that I find a fiancée, and that's what I did. I never imagined it would blow up like this."

"If we would've known about her past, we could've worked with this, made it a real asset." Caroline began. "We could have at least been prepared."

"If you would've asked me anything about her, you would've known. None of you cared about anything having to do with Lily except the fact that she'd agreed to marry me. Don't put this all on me. And Lily's fairly private about her first marriage. I doubt she'd appreciate her tragic loss being used as a campaign asset."

Beneath his indignation, Ford knew that he should have been forthright with them about Lily's first husband. That information was much too big to keep to himself. She surely would've objected to bringing him into the campaign, though, and he didn't want unnecessary tension between them. He also knew that the team was right: the widow of an American hero was a powerful asset. As long as Lily kept her first marriage private, though, it was easier for him not to think about how she'd once been married to someone she'd chosen. Someone she'd fought to be with. Someone he could never live up to.

"What can we do now, then? I'm sure we can somehow convince people that she supports the military, spin it, or distance ourselves from her father. I doubt the fact that she's a widow will bother people. They might even like her more."

"If we'd had the information from the beginning, we could have presented Lily as a sympathetic figure. We could have romanced the voters with her story of heartbreak and the new love she's found in you. But we didn't know in time, and we're in trouble because now we lost our chance to be proactive. Everything we put out there about Lily is a reaction at this point. It's not her first husband that can sink us. It's her father and the way she appears to agree with his critical view of the military's treatment of widows and veterans," Caroline answered. "And this is a lot to overcome." She waved her hand over the printouts and images on the screens. "I'm not sure simply stating that she doesn't fully agree with her father is going to help."

Okay, that was true, but Lily herself wasn't the one blasting the military, and he had to believe that the situation could still be salvaged. "I was there, guys, and Lily seemed pro-military to me. She was honest about the struggles faced by the people they want to serve, but she didn't knock the army. If anything, I'd think the fact that she lost her husband to war and still remains positive about the military looks great for us."

"Ford, she didn't dispute or object to one thing her father said in that interview. Regardless of what she may truly think about our nation's military and their treatment of veterans and widows, sitting by idly during his rant showed viewers that Lily agrees with him. People believe what they want, and more often than not, they want to think the worst." Charlie sounded more resigned than angry. "I mean, for heaven's sake, did he have to bring up PTSD and soldier suicide rates? It wasn't even noon! I was under the impression that they were going on-air for a light-hearted and informative interview. He turned it into his own private protest."

As much as he'd hoped that the whole thing would blow over, Ford had to agree with their assessment. Lily's father was passionate in his beliefs, and he did a lot of good for those he worked with, but he was controversial and confrontational. Blowing out a frustrated breath, he leaned forward, elbows on the table. "What do we do now? What's next?"

Robert spoke up first. "We'd like for Lily to come in for a meeting. If you'll set it up, we'll devise a plan to spin this in our favor, do some damage control. We have to get her on board, and you're the only one who can do that."

"We hope it's not too late to fix this," added Charlie. "This is a major snag. And that's putting it mildly."

The expression on each face circling the table was the same: resignation mixed with disappointment. Knowing that he was responsible, through his inaction or omission, whatever it was that made him think that Lily's past was unimportant to the campaign, Ford vowed to make it right. Too many people had dedicated the past several months of their lives to his re-election to leave anything else to chance.

"Okay, then. I'll talk to Lily, and Joelle will schedule the meeting. We'll be here, and we'll be ready to follow your plan. I trust that you'll figure this out, and I'll do whatever I can to fix this. Anything else?" With a heavy sigh, he sat back in his chair and met the eyes of each of his team members, challenging them to continue.

Caroline snapped her notebook closed. "Nope. If you get Ms. Ashton in here to meet with us, we'll figure out the rest."

• • •

Lily parked her car in Ford's campaign headquarters parking lot, and Ford met her before she even had time to kill the engine. His handsome face held the worry she'd heard in his voice when he called for her to meet him. He motioned that he'd like to join her in the car and jogged around to the passenger side. He dropped into the seat, leaning over to give her a quick kiss on the cheek.

"Thanks for coming over so quickly. The team is freaking out."

Her shoulders slumped. "I was afraid of that. What about you?"

He flashed her a smile, projecting a confidence that surprised her. "Don't worry about me. Or us."

"I had no idea my dad was going to say all those things. I hope it's not causing too much trouble."

Ford sat back in his seat. "It's not helping, obviously, but I'm sure the team will think of some way to handle it. They're very good at what they do."

"The thing is, I agree with him on most points. I wish he hadn't chosen morning television as his platform, but his opinions are valid. I'm worried that I don't fit into the mold your campaign has set for you."

He took her hand in his and squeezed. "We'll face things like this many times in our life together. Every time I run for office, at least, and probably even when I'm not. What's important is that we stick together and support one another."

"Okay." She let out a big breath. Handling a crisis so soon into their engagement was not something Lily had anticipated, but she was in it now. "Let's do this."

. . .

Ford led Lily through the campaign office, smiling at his staff and trying to ignore the curious stares. He held the conference room door open for her, and his team rose from their chairs to greet her.

Caroline leaned forward first, clearing her throat and extending a hand. After some pleasantries and making sure Lily remembered everyone, Caroline gestured to one of the empty chairs and invited her to join the group. An intern wheeled in a tray bearing coffee, water, soft drinks, and pastries. Ford took his seat next to Lily and tried to lighten the mood.

"I'm going to start bringing you to all our strategy meetings. I usually have to make do with whatever drink I can remember to bring in with me." The team laughed politely, not meeting his eye as they shuffled papers and readied themselves for the meeting.

"Thanks for coming in on such short notice." Charlie nodded to the intern as she set a cup of coffee in front of him. "I wish you were here under more pleasant circumstances, but we'll do the best we can to make this quick and painless. Let's get down to it."

Lily sat up straighter, and Ford wished he could ease her tension. She was smart and self-possessed, independent and confident, but being called in to a congressional campaign advisory team meeting to address a problem they basically thought was her fault was likely outside of her wheelhouse. Last time they'd been here together, the conversation and strategizing was almost exciting, like solving a problem as a team; this time was more like being called to the principal's office. When Coldwell went on the offensive, things were rough, but at least they could direct their frustration at him.

Caroline opened a folder and pulled out the contents, pushing pictures of Lily's parents at protests in the '80s. Ford flipped through them and had to smile at one with a baby Lily sleeping peacefully in a stroller as her parents raised signs with anti-war slogans scrawled across them in bold black letters. Her mother, eyes focused and intense, shouted while her sign proclaimed "Women are People!" in black block letters. Ted's sign, held aloft with the hand not resting on Lily's stroller handle, said "The GOP Assault on Women is IMMORAL." Ford sucked in a breath, not sure what the Ashtons were protesting but knowing there wasn't much they could do to spin it. Why were there so many of these, and why did he have to be so specific?

"There are plenty more, but you get the idea." Charlie's face was grim as he looked from Lily to Ford.

Lily shifted nervously in her chair, and Ford took her hand under the table and squeezed. "Surely, my fiancée's parents' political activity in the eighties can't be that big a deal, can it? It's not as though they're out every weekend marching on City Hall. Besides, none of these are very recent. I haven't seen anything that looks like it's not at least twenty years old. And Lily's not participating in any of them."

"Sure, under normal circumstances, we could ignore this kind of thing or at least downplay it if Coldwell dug it up. Nothing is really off-limits when it comes to a race this close, but we could've managed it. The problem is that Mr. Ashton was just on live television, criticizing our nation's military when you're in the heat of a re-election campaign. He's stirred up enough interest to dredge up the past. Put it all together, and it paints a pretty bleak picture." Diana Harris, Ford's most serious advisor, spoke up. "Sam Coldwell's campaign is having a field day with this. We've already seen how quickly he moves when it comes to your relationship with Ms. Ashton. Combine her father's outburst with the abundance of photographs from their apparently prolific protest appearances, and it's the perfect storm."

Her eyes fixed on Ford's, and Robert cleared his throat. "And then there's this."

He turned his tablet around so that the screen was facing Ford and Lily. The much-circulated photograph of Lily at her first husband's funeral was on the screen with a blog headline that read: "Congressman's Fiancée's Troubled Military Past."

Lily's hand flew to her mouth, and her eyes filled with tears. Ford had seen the picture dozens of times since the interview, but he realized in that moment that she probably hadn't seen it since it was new. More than anything, he wished he'd prepared her for the meeting better.

"Turn that off." He bit out the words, quietly but firmly.

Robert had the grace to appear chastened as he flipped the screen around to face him and averted his eyes. "I'm sorry, Ms. Ashton. I suppose we've had more time to process this development than you have. We should have better prepared you."

With a deep breath, Lily folded her hands in her lap and sat up before meeting the gaze of the team members circling the table. "No, it's fine. It's certainly not your fault that some other candidate is using my personal tragedy for political gain. That picture was everywhere after the funeral. I just haven't seen it since then, and it was a shock. Really, you don't have to tiptoe around me."

The team members visibly relaxed, but their expressions remained serious. Charlie broke the silence. "The Coldwell campaign has implied that you are in agreement with your father when it comes to his anti-military views. They're citing the loss of your first husband as proof that you blame the government and military for the tragic end of your first marriage."

"Seriously? That's ridiculous. I've never said anything publicly about my husband's death, and I've certainly never blamed anyone." Lily sounded genuinely surprised, though Ford had often wondered himself if Lily might hold some resentment toward the military. It was only natural, and no one would fault her if she did.

"Unfortunately," Charlie answered with a sober nod, "it's an easy conclusion to draw, and he's not wasting any time using this to his advantage. Your silence might as well confirm their assertions, so it's imperative that we move quickly to squelch them."

"I am and always have been a steadfast supporter of this country and of the men and women who serve us in the military. Nathan believed in what he was doing and spoke of that conviction often in the letters he sent to me during his deployment. He had a mission, and he was proud to carry it out with his fellow soldiers, knowing in his heart that what they were doing was absolutely right. He never wavered in that, never once showed fear or any misgivings." She paused, took a sip of water, and continued. "He was loyal to this country, gave everything for this country. To him, their mission was vital, and he never looked back. I've never once believed any differently."

"Ma'am, I think the fact that he has never been mentioned during this campaign makes it look like we have something to hide." Robert avoided eye contact with Lily, likely humbled by her impassioned speech.

"You people have a plan for handling every other aspect of my life. Why was this one overlooked?" Her voice rose an octave, and her jaw flexed as she waited for their answers. "I'm honestly surprised that you didn't use this information to your advantage."

"We didn't have the information until the interview." Robert answered Lily's question but kept his eyes on Ford. "None of us knew you'd been married before, much less under these circumstances."

"What? You didn't vet me like your file folder bride candidates? Ford didn't ever mention him?" The edge of hysteria tinged her voice, and Ford wished more than ever that he could go back and do everything differently. "It's a pretty big detail to leave out, don't you think?"

"Ma'am, Ford did not give us the information, and you were not fully vetted because you were his personal choice. We trusted that he was making the best decision for himself and didn't get involved. We only have the information that you've given us because we didn't dig into your personal life." Robert answered with a soothing tone, lowering his voice and trying to bring the mood back to normal.

"I didn't realize you could use my loss for the campaign, so I never offered it. Sorry." Her tone was steely with sarcasm, her voice low. She looked straight ahead, refusing to meet his eye.

"I'm sure that's not what they're implying," Ford spoke up, hoping that they weren't suggesting that the opportunistic hijacking of Lily's private pain was to be met with any response from his team other than to shame them. He placed a tentative hand on her knee under the table, hoping to make a connection and show of support, but she flinched away from his touch.

"We certainly don't want to exploit your private life like the Coldwell campaign has done, but we don't see how this can go without an answer," said Caroline. "We've got to do something."

"What did you have in mind?" Ford asked, not entirely sure Lily would stay in her seat long enough to hear. She looked both furious and heartbroken, and he was sorry to have dragged her into the situation. He hoped like hell that the team had a foolproof idea on how to get them out of this without hurting her any more.

"We have a few options, but the best is to make a big push toward repairing your public image immediately. Ideally, we'd like to arrange for another interview on *Good Morning, Dallas* to give the voters a chance to get to know Ms. Ashton more intimately. We've been in contact with the show's writers and feel confident that they would be sensitive to Lily's situation and treat her with the utmost respect." Caroline faced Lily. "If you'd be willing to talk about your first marriage, let the viewers know that your husband believed in his mission and you supported it, we believe that could go a long way in repairing this. We have to stop pretending that Ford is the first man you've ever loved and bring this out in the open."

"I've never spoken about Nathan in public, and I don't want to start now. It feels dirty to use him to help Ford's campaign. I know we have a public relationship, but some things should be private." Lily's shoulders slumped, the fire gone.

As though knowing it was inappropriate but unable to stop herself from asking, Caroline gently suggested more. "Perhaps we could see the letters he wrote you? Show the people how he spoke about his country and his mission? Maybe another interview with you isn't absolutely necessary. We could work with the show to produce a segment about your husband."

"That's out of the question, and I'm shocked that you would even ask. Those are personal and not available for public consumption. Had I known this was part of the deal, that you people were basically running a circus, I don't think I would've agreed to be a part of this campaign. Excuse me." Her voice was cold and hard as steel, a tone Ford had never heard her use.

Standing and pushing her chair back behind her hard enough that Ford had to catch it in her wake, Lily stormed out of the room, letting the door fly closed behind her. The team sat, stunned into silence around the table, until Ford snapped out of his shock and realized he should follow her.

"Having Lily involved is the only chance we have at mending this thing. How could you sit there with a straight face and ask to see her dead husband's letters? What the hell is wrong with you?" Without waiting for an answer, he rushed out to catch Lily before she left.

• • •

"Lily, wait!" Ford called out as she rushed toward her car. He hurried toward her, stopping short of getting hit by a BMW exiting the lot.

She whipped around to face him, shielding her eyes from the setting sun. "What?"

He paused at her tone, unsure what to say once he stopped her. He'd never seen her like this, and it was frightening. For their first disagreement ever, this was major. With his hands raised in surrender, he crossed the parking lot and closed the distance between them. "I'm sorry about everything. Can we talk about it?"

"I don't see what else there is to say. Your team is out of their damn minds, and I'm done. I'm not doing what they ask, so if you still want to win, you've got to let me go and try this on your own. It's probably your best chance, if not the only one." A tear escaped her eye, and she wiped it away with the back of her hand. "This is too much. Nobody talks much about these campaign scandals after they're over. Something new will come up, and everyone will move on with the news cycle. Everyone but me, I mean. I'll be destroyed, and then it will be forgotten by everyone else. If I allow myself to get caught up in this, I don't think I'll get over it."

"Honey, I'll make sure you're treated with nothing but respect. We don't have to do anything you don't want to do." She stiffened when he wrapped his arms around her, but he held tight and rubbed her back. "I care about you, and I don't want to see you get hurt."

She sniffled and pressed her cheek to his chest. "Thank you."

Not sure how he'd protect her and his own interests, but certain he didn't want to let her go, he squeezed tighter. Pressing his lips against her hair and inhaling deeply, he searched for a solution.

"What can we do?" he murmured into her hair.

She stiffened again and pulled back, out of his embrace. Shaking his hands off her arms, her face fell. "I don't want to have anything to do with this. I wasn't kidding in there. I've been feeling normal for the first time in a long time, and bringing Nathan into this campaign would change everything." With a shuddering breath, her eyes reflected a profound sadness. "It's not going away, is it?"

He dropped his hands, shoulders slumped. "Come on, Lily. We can't simply ignore it. I want to protect you, and I don't want you to get hurt, but I can't make it go away. There's no way around it."

"Then leave me out of it and move on with your life and your campaign. This engagement was never about us; it was about you and what you need. I think having a liberal, anti-military fiancée is worse than not having one at all, don't you?"

"That's not fair, and you know it. If you'll let us do something to change the public's perception of you, they'll realize that you're not anti-military. They'll see who I see, someone who is patriotic and optimistic despite everything that's happened. You have to give us a chance, though. It's unreasonable to refuse to do anything to address the problem and expect it to work itself out."

Fire flashed in her eyes, the vulnerability replaced with anger. "No, what's unreasonable is to expect me to go through something so painful for nothing in return. You're the one who stands to gain from this, Ford, not me. I'm not the one running for office."

"Let's do this together, please. It's not all about me, Lily. I want you to be happy. I want to make you happy." The pleading in his voice was obvious, but he pressed forward. She wasn't bending, and he was dangerously close to losing everything. He could lose the election, but worse, he could lose her. "I'm so grateful to you for agreeing to the engagement, but I thought it was something special for you, too. I know you started this as a favor to me, but it's more than that now. I'm not imagining that."

"No, you're not imagining things. It was becoming more. Now I'm not so sure."

"Come on. Don't throw what we could have together over some temporary discomfort. Please." He tried to take her hands, to make a connection, but she refused.

"Discomfort? Try devastation, humiliation, and heartbreak. Can you even hear yourself when you speak?"

"I'm not trying to minimize it, just trying to get you to see the big picture. All I meant was that we can do this together, like the team we'll be when we're married. It may be uncomfortable, but with the team's help, we can strategize. You'll be able to confront the situation with support behind you. You won't be alone in this."

"You don't get it, and I don't know any other way to tell you. I'm done, and there's no way I'm using my personal life to help you win this election." The anger that fueled her was replaced with resignation. "I'm not part of your campaign strategy. I'm not even sure I'll vote for you at this point."

With a sad smile, she twisted her engagement ring off her finger and pressed it into his palm, got in her car, and closed the door without another word. As she drove off, Ford stood helplessly and watched her disappear into the busy traffic, taking his chances of re-election with her. Losing her was what gutted him, though. How she had managed to turn their arrangement into something he couldn't live without was astounding. And he'd lost everything before he realized what he had with her.

When he finally turned back toward the office, he saw Charlie standing behind him, close enough to hear everything. Having an audience made the whole thing so much worse, and the last thing he wanted to do was share the moment with that man. "How long have you been out here?"

"Only a few seconds. I was heading to my car and stopped when I saw you two." Charlie had trouble meeting his eyes.

"Well, that's great." His voice dripped with sarcasm, and he didn't even attempt to be professional. "I'm sure Lily loved having an audience for that, seeing as how much she loves having my campaign team involved in her personal business."

"Honestly, Ford. I didn't hear a single word of your conversation. It really was only a few seconds." He cringed, and added, "I got out here right as she was returning your engagement ring."

"Well, you're the one who decided I should get married in the first place. It's only fitting that you should be here to see it fall apart, too, I guess." Ford knew it wasn't Charlie's fault, or the team's fault, that he'd landed in this mess. He could've gone a different way, refused to follow their plan, or handled Lily's situation differently. He could only blame himself. Targeting them was so much more satisfying, though.

"Ford, I know it's hard right now, but if she's this resistant already, when things are relatively easy, do you think she'd stick around for the long haul? What do you think she'd do if we found ourselves with a real problem? This one is tough, but we had a simple, straightforward solution, and she refused to even consider helping you. I think you might have dodged a bullet."

Instead of figuring out how to fix the problem, possibly bring her back into the fold, his advisor was glad to have the obstacle removed. To him, Lily was a piece of the puzzle, nothing more, and if she wasn't going to fit, then it was best to find out early. With as much heartbreak that had come with allowing others to interfere with his life in the past, how had Ford managed to let it happen again? Disgusted with himself, he knew he'd gotten what he deserved. Again. He'd come so far since he'd allowed his mother to manipulate him into breaking it off with his first love. Apparently all it took was a simple setback and he was right back where he started.

"Screw you, Charlie." He stormed into the office to get his keys, bumping into Charlie in his haste but not looking back.

Chapter Ten

The following afternoon, Lily opened the door to Michael Welch's bakery, The Clubhouse, to a burst of loud music and vanilla-scented air. Carly's own bakery, Caketopia, was decidedly more posh and sophisticated, but today they were working together at Michael's place. Carly was leaning against the counter, flipping through a catalog with an employee. "I don't care what people are pinning on Pinterest. We are not keeping these in stock. If you have to tie up a man and drag him to the altar, he's not someone you should marry. I just don't think these are clever." Lily could see cake toppers picturing brides pulling grooms by their collars and had to laugh. Typical Carly.

She looked up from the counter and grinned, nearly toppling over her metal barstool in her haste to get to Lily. The pair met in the middle of the storefront's glossy black floor and hugged. She'd only been gone a short while, but with everything that had happened, it felt like forever.

"I'm so glad you're back!" Lily couldn't stop a few happy tears from falling. She'd missed her best friend, and she couldn't have returned from her honeymoon soon enough. Going through the business with Ford and his campaign without her friend there to help had been torture. Carly took Lily's left hand, and her excitement turned to bewilderment when she didn't find an engagement ring.

"Where's your ring?" Carly looked up at her, concern replacing the joy they'd felt at their reunion. "What happened?"

"What didn't happen?" Lily let out a shuddering breath. "Things have fallen apart in spectacular fashion. It's over."

"Come with me." Carly instructed the employee to keep an eye on the front and led Lily through a swinging door. The atmosphere behind the wild storefront, which was outfitted to appear more like a grown-up clubhouse than a bakery, was markedly more generic and professional. They found an empty workroom and pulled up stools to the pristine stainless steel table that dominated the room.

"I should've grabbed some cupcakes from the case. You want me to run back? Something tells me this is one of those situations that call for sugar." Carly swung one leg over the stool, ready to run back up to the front.

Lily attempted a laugh, but it sounded more like a hiccup. "No, that's fine. Some things can't be fixed with cake and frosting."

Carly put a hand over heart, swaying dramatically. "If I believed that, I don't see what the point of living would be." She patted Lily's hand. "I'm sorry. What's going on? Tell me everything."

"It's over between me and Ford. Things were going so well, and it unraveled so fast. After we got engaged, everything really came together for us. It was weird but wonderful how much closer we got and how quickly. I mean, for a while, I thought I might actually be in love with him." Lily sighed and looked around the room, wishing she could share the whole story of their engagement. "Then my dad and I did an interview on *Good Morning, Dallas* about Soldier On, and things went downhill from there. Everything just fell apart."

She told Carly about how the picture of her at Nathan's funeral popping up everywhere and how Ford's team wanted her to use her story to shore up the campaign. The more she explained, the more she realized she'd made the right decision. She couldn't marry a man who didn't accept her past, who wouldn't stand up for her. If he was going to put his campaign ahead of her now, what would he do further down the line?

Carly rubbed her shoulder in sympathy. "Aw, honey, I'm so sorry. I hate that you're going through this, and I support you no matter what happens. But this whole thing fell apart in one afternoon? Is there any chance you didn't give Ford the chance to do the right thing? I doubt he let you go without even trying to fix things."

Lily stiffened. She'd been so caught up in her righteous indignation that she never stopped to consider that Ford wasn't necessarily a bad guy. Still, the situation was bleak. "He had the chance to make things right, or at least promise to. I mean, he wasn't even angry on my behalf."

"So, he didn't react how you hoped. Think it through, though. Was he on board with his campaign team, or was he protective of you?"

"It happened so fast; everything spiraled out of control. He seemed to understand why I was upset, but he tried to figure out a way to keep me happy but still get what he needed for the campaign. When I realized that the whole thing was about him and what he wanted, regardless of how I'd be affected, I knew it was over."

Maybe she should've given him the benefit of the doubt, or at least a chance to think before reacting. His initial reaction had to be the one that counted, though. His instinct should be to protect her, to side with her no matter what, and his first concern was to follow his team's edict and safeguard his precious campaign. Her gut told her that his first reaction was the best way to see his true nature. Comparing him to Nathan was unhealthy, and she knew it, but it was inevitable. Maybe she'd been spoiled by her first marriage, but she needed to be her husband's first priority, needed to know that he'd be willing to do anything to defend her. Nathan had taught her what it was like to be treasured. The trouble with Ford's campaign made her feel like an asset that wasn't performing well.

"It's over, whether I should've given it more time or not. I can't very well call him and ask for the ring back. I might have been hasty, but it's better to get out now that I know where I stand."

"I just hate that you finally took a chance and this happened." Carly stood and pushed her stool under the table before heading for the door. "It won't solve anything, but we definitely need those cupcakes."

• • •

Ford pulled out his mother's chair for her and waited as she sat. The busy restaurant's lunch crowd filled the space with chatter, the clinking of silverware against plates, and a backdrop to share his latest failure. He took his seat across from her and accepted a menu from the hostess.

"This is an unexpected pleasure." Mother scanned her menu and eyed him over the top, her eyes searching for the reason they were meeting for lunch.

"I wanted to see you before I head back to D.C." He tried for a light, casual tone, but his stomach turned at the thought of what he was about to tell her.

"Well then, darling, count me doubly flattered. I know you have a quick turnaround before you'll be back home for Election Day, but I would've thought you'd be splitting your time between your campaign and Lily."

They'd discussed a canceled engagement of his before, but last time it was a victory for her. She'd had such a hand in ending his relationship that he could rest on his anger and ignore his responsibility. It was years after the fact before he could even admit to himself that he'd been culpable at all. This time, he'd failed on his own, even going so far as to forbid her to interfere, so everything rested squarely on his shoulders. Lily hadn't returned his calls, and he'd been forced to accept that he'd be returning to D.C. without making things right with her. Best to let Mother know before he left town, to get it over with. Charlie and his father were incredibly close; it was only a matter of time before Charlie mentioned it.

They ordered lunch, and he briefly wondered if he should join Mother and have a midday Chardonnay as well, or maybe something stronger. She handed her menu to the waiter and fixed Ford with an expectant look. Not one to be fooled with flattery, she knew there was more to the visit than a simple meal before he left town.

No use prolonging the inevitable. "Lily and I have called off the engagement."

One sentence summed up the entire situation but didn't tell even half the story. To her credit, Mother didn't even let the tiniest hint of a smile tug at her lips before composing her expression into one of compassion. "Oh, dear, I'm so sorry. What happened?"

"I'm sure you've seen some of the news coverage about her that came out after she and her dad went on *Good Morning, Dallas*. Things got heated when we met with the campaign team to discuss our plans to deal with the fallout. We couldn't come to an agreement, and she decided to end things."

"Just like that? I'd think your fiancée would be more supportive of you." The drinks arrived, and she took a tiny sip of her wine.

"There are complicated issues about her first husband and her politics. The news came out that she herself is a military widow, and there are all these opinions flying around about her feelings about the military. It's not as simple as being supportive of me."

"I knew she looked familiar. I remember seeing those pictures of her at the funeral everywhere after that young man died. I couldn't quite place her, though. Why didn't you mention any of this?" He'd been asking himself that same question all day.

She accepted her meal from the waiter with a cursory nod and spread her napkin in her lap. After everything that had happened, Ford couldn't think of one good reason to have handled Lily's past the way he did. Perhaps he'd wished for a simpler relationship, one where he wasn't competing with a husband gone before he could disappoint her. One where he wasn't being compared to someone brave, strong, and grounded in his convictions. Maybe he knew everyone would have an opinion about using the information and didn't want to address it until forced. Probably a combination of many reasons, none of them good enough to justify his behavior. He chewed his tasteless meal as he thought about what he'd done.

"She's incredibly private about her first marriage, and I didn't want to make her uncomfortable. I worried that everyone would ask her about her husband, so I tried to give her at least a little time to adjust to having her life being an open book instead of forcing her to face it all at once." He shrugged. He had no good defense for his actions, but there was nothing he could do to change the past. "I didn't realize that it would come out so quickly. I should have managed this better."

"Really, Ford, I don't know how you get yourself into these situations." She took a delicate bite of radish from her salad and chewed thoughtfully. "Perhaps it's best that you got out before anything worse happened."

"What do you mean?" She sounded like Charlie, but when she said it, he could only blame himself.

"Honestly, she's a beautiful young woman, but did you really think she was an appropriate choice for you? Listen, I know you don't want to hear anything I have to say about your love life, but you need a certain kind of woman by your side if you're going to be successful. Lily's not exactly congressman's wife material, much less governor's wife."

"I can't believe we're doing this again." He'd let it happen, and he was thoroughly disgusted with himself.

She feigned innocence. "I did exactly as you asked and kept my mouth shut, as promised. I'm simply glad that you figured out this wouldn't work before things went any further with that one."

"That one? Mother, please. We are talking about my fiancée, the woman I love." Though he'd never admitted it to himself or said it to Lily, buckling under the full force of losing her made him realize that he did, in fact, love her.

At the admission, her face softened. She set her fork on her plate and gave him a sad smile. "Darling, I didn't realize. I thought you proposed because your team advised it. I'm sorry." Her hand covered his for a moment, more contact than he was used to from her, and she continued. "I've always tried to protect you, but apparently it wasn't Lily you needed to worry about. Do you remember your Uncle Monroe?"

"Of course. Well, vaguely." His father's younger brother died when Ford was probably ten or eleven years old. He had a few memories of him from holidays, vacations, and time spent on the golf course with his dad, but nothing specific.

"When he was a bit younger than you are, he met a beautiful young lady, Michelle. She was absolutely stunning, and he couldn't resist giving her everything she wanted. They were married very quickly after they met, and we never got to know her very well." The waiter arrived to check on them, and she waved him away with a smile. "She wasn't around long enough, as it turned out. Michelle made sure that they never spent much time with us, and he was so in love with her that he didn't argue about it. They were married maybe a year, if that, when everything started to fall apart. She cheated on your uncle, spent money like it was water, and treated him like dirt. She finally filed for divorce, and it was ugly. She was ruthless: telling him she'd never loved him, hiding her jewelry and expensive gifts, and fighting tooth and nail for every last dollar she could get out of him."

"I had no idea." Ford felt horrible for his uncle, but he wasn't sure what that had to do with his situation.

"So, eventually, the whole story came out. Michelle had married him for his money and didn't care how she got it. She definitely didn't care who got hurt in the process." Mother took a sip of wine. "He was ruined, absolutely ruined. After she left, he started drinking heavily, stopped caring about work, wouldn't see us. It was truly heartbreaking."

"That's awful." The connection was becoming clearer, but he didn't think he and Lily had a similar story. She supported herself and had never once mentioned money.

"Nobody could reach him, and then, well, you know how that ended."

He'd died in a one-person fatal car accident when he wrapped his car around a tree after drinking himself into a stupor. Ford would never forget the night his parents got the call, the confusion he felt in the days following the accident, or the funeral. His parents had kept most of the details from him and his brothers, probably both caught up in their own sorrow and unsure how to address such heavy matters with such young boys. It was only when he was older that he learned what really happened to his uncle, and then it was only the most basic information.

"I wanted to protect you and your brothers from having the same thing happen to you. Money does strange things to people, and you can never tell for sure when motivations are true. I thought the best way to prevent a similar situation would be to eliminate the possibility. I thought if we stuck with families that we know, or if you'd at least choose someone who came from a bit of money herself, then it would at least help. I'm truly sorry for not trusting you to make your own choices."

Ford took a long drink from his water, absorbing the information. Mother had never opened up to him before, had certainly never apologized or admitted that she could be wrong. He tamped down the initial flare of anger. She'd manipulated him purposefully and waited too long to let him in on her plan. However, she'd traveled well out of her comfort zone to admit everything to him today, and ultimately, her actions were motivated by love. He couldn't blame everything on her forever, either; her interference and disapproval didn't cause his behavior. It was time he owned up to that. He blew out a heavy breath and looked at his mother for who she really was: a deeply flawed woman who loved him.

"I wish I'd known, but it's not your fault I lost Lily."

A smile cracked the stillness that had settled over her while she waited for his reaction. "I'm sorry I didn't tell you sooner, and I'm sorry that Lily left. Do you think there's a chance she'll reconsider?"

Here he was, once again, having lost the chance at happiness because he'd been too spineless to stand up for his woman. Nobody wholeheartedly supported their engagement, and it should have solidified their relationship, brought them closer together as they fought for each other. Instead, he'd crumpled under pressure, had taken the easy way out and tried to pacify everyone. Everyone but the one person who really mattered. She was gone, and she was right to protect herself, because lord knows he wasn't man enough to do it. If there was a chance she'd reconsider, he'd be surprised.

"I seriously doubt it, Mother. I've tried to get in touch with her, but she completely refuses to have any contact with me."

"I hope you think of some way to get through to her. I really do, if that's what you truly want. I will stay out of it from now on. I'm sure you can take care of yourself, and I probably shouldn't have interfered."

They finished their meal, conversation a bit strained after the heavy revelations, but ultimately in comfortable companionship. It had taken far too long, but finally having Mother reveal her human side and treat him like an adult was worth the wait. He only wished he had more time left before he had to head back to D.C. for a few days. It was a terrible time to be leaving, but he'd already ruined his relationship. No need to ruin his job as well.

Chapter Eleven

Yawning and struggling to shake the sleep out of his head and focus, Ford stretched at his desk in his D.C. office. He'd had coffee at his apartment and another on the way into work, but nothing could drag him out of the fog. After arriving on an evening flight, he'd had a quick dinner alone and spent a sleepless night thinking of Lily. After a dozen calls she wouldn't answer, a handful of voicemails, and a few emails, he admitted defeat. She'd seen the truth and didn't want any part of him or his stupid campaign. Of course he couldn't go back and undo what happened, and now it was impossible to take his team's advice and keep emotions out of the engagement by going with one of their choices. There would be no fiancée, no convenient answer to his opponent's criticism, and there was nothing he could do about it this late in the game. In one swift motion, he'd screwed up his personal and professional life.

His team had decided to cut their losses and make the simple, straightforward announcement that he and Lily had decided to end their engagement. They hoped that if they refused any further discussion, she wouldn't reveal the truth behind the scheme. He couldn't fulfill the fiancée portion of their strategy on the heels of his breakup, so they were counting on voters' sympathy to gloss over the issue of his bachelor status. With a week left until Election Night, there was nothing left to do but hit the campaign hard. They'd be working back home on his behalf, and he'd split his time between his congressional duties and trying to win last minute votes. It would be the longest week of his life, but he doubted he'd get much rest anyway.

An email popped up with drafts of his victory and concession speeches, ready for his approval or changes. For a moment, he stared at the little American flag on his desk and remembered the exhilaration of winning his last election, trying to summon a modicum of that enthusiasm. Nothing. Imagining a victory, then a defeat, he waited for a rush of excitement or devastation to wash over him, but there was only a gnawing emptiness in his gut. Nothing mattered without Lily, and he wasn't ready to face the rest of his life without her. The way things stood, she wasn't interested in having anything to do with him. His team was hard at work in constructing his post-engagement plan, and they wouldn't support any reconciliation attempt.

And then it hit him.

Everything he'd done to destroy his relationship was in reaction to the opinions and desires of others, just like the first time. He knew that, but wallowing in self-loathing wasn't getting him anywhere. The first time he'd let someone else decide his future, he was young and inexperienced, clearly not ready to be man enough to handle the responsibilities of an adult relationship. Now there was no excuse, and he was ready to fight, to stand up for himself and his relationship, to fight for the woman he loved. If it wasn't going to work out, it was going to be between the two of them this time, no one else.

Deciding to take responsibility for his own life, to move forward with purpose, gave way to that rush of optimism and enthusiasm he'd waited for. He wanted to win the election, but he had to win Lily back. Without knowing he'd fought for her, he didn't want anything else. His advisors wouldn't like what he was going to do next, but he wasn't doing it for them.

•••

After work, a grueling outdoor photo shoot where Lily tried to pretend wearing a bikini in November was exactly what she wanted to be doing, she drove to Michael's apartment. Carly had moved in with him while they decided where they were going to live permanently, and Lily had never been to his place before. Having known of Michael's bad boy reputation before getting to know him through Carly, she was curious about where the reality television star lived.

Carly answered the door and led her into a disappointingly normal-looking apartment. Where was the leather furniture and giant flat screen television? He didn't have a fully stocked bar dominating the living area? No obnoxious neon beer sign? And the air smelled like cinnamon and chocolate, not cigarette smoke and stale booze. Michael Welch was a normal guy. What a letdown.

"Michael is out tonight having dinner with Jenny, but he made us a cake this afternoon. It's a new chocolate cinnamon flavor he's trying to perfect. I promised him we'd try every version of the recipe until he got it just right." Jenny was Michael's younger sister who lived in an assisted living facility. She'd become accustomed to Michael being away after he and Carly started traveling for their hit television show, but they always needed time to catch up when he returned. They were rarely out of town for as long as they'd been in Paris for the honeymoon, so chances were good that he'd be gone all evening and Lily would have Carly all to herself.

Since Ford left town, she'd been alternately tempted to burrow under her blankets and sleep until she forgot him and to forgive everything so they could be together. He'd called, emailed, and texted, but she couldn't bring herself to respond. Nothing he could say would make it better, not until he was truly willing to prioritize her and their relationship could they move forward. She couldn't go on playing nothing more than a piece in the puzzle.

Carly picked up her phone. "And Michael just texted me that there's something we need to watch on the DVR." She shrugged and set the phone on the table. "Let's get some cake, then we'll see what he's got in store for us."

Lily followed Carly through the apartment and sat on a barstool, leaning on the counter that separated the kitchen from the living area. Carly pulled plates out of the cabinets and grabbed a couple of forks from the drawer. A magazine-perfect cake sat on a pedestal plate, almost too beautiful to cut into. Carly had no problem destroying it though, as she saw cakes like that every day. She cut two thick slices for them and slid one plate across the bar to Lily. "This goes great with red wine, but we have milk, too, if you want."

Lily laughed. A glass of milk wouldn't begin to scratch the surface of her pain. "Milk has never solved anybody's problems. I think I'm going to need the wine."

Carly handed her two empty glasses and pulled a bottle from their wine rack. "I figured as much. Come on, let's start your therapy."

They settled in at the coffee table, sitting on oversized pillows. Lily leaned back against the couch, the first bite of Michael's cake melting in her mouth.

"I can see why you married him. This is seriously the best thing I've ever tasted. It's so freaking good." With a happy sigh, she took another bite and let herself relax for the first time since she'd broken up with Ford. The world had crumbled around her, but with her best friend and the amazing cake, she could survive yet. "I might just marry this cake. It would never let me down."

Carly topped off their wine glasses and tucked her feet underneath her. "I'm so sorry about Ford. I wish there were something I could do to help."

Finally spending time with her friend and talking about the breakup would help a little. Lily knew that time was the only thing that could heal her, though, unless Ford magically found a way to go back in time, undo the damage he'd caused, and fix everything. "This cake is a good start, but there's nothing anyone can do. Ford was the only one who could've changed anything about the way things went, and he didn't. I needed him to be there for me in a way that he obviously just can't be. Now I just have to get through it." Lily set her fork down on the plate, feeling the full weight of her sadness and almost choking on the misery. "I kept thinking, through all of this, that he would stand up for me, that he'd put us and our relationship above everything else, if only for a moment. Maybe I have unrealistic expectations of what a husband should be, but I just needed that one thing from him. I really thought he would, and when he didn't, when everyone else was more important than me, it killed me."

Carly was her biggest champion, but she also had a knack for seeing things from every angle. "Is it possible that you overreacted? He couldn't just drop everything and do exactly what you wanted, could he? I mean, I agree that he should put your relationship first, and I'm totally on your side, of course." She put her hands up, apparently expecting Lily to react negatively. "All I'm saying is that he has at least some obligation to his campaign, doesn't he?"

Lily sneered at her friend playfully. "Quit trying to make sense and just take my side. What kind of best friend are you, anyway?" She took a big bite of cake and considered Carly's words. Their engagement came about purely as a machination of the campaign machine. Should she have been so surprised when it ended the way it did? Was Carly right? Was she overreacting?

Carly picked up the remote control and turned the television on. "I'm just trying to help you see it from another perspective. If you want to wallow in your righteous anger, I'll be there with you. Let's see what Michael left for us."

"If he's trying for a romantic surprise for you and it's the engagement episode of your show, I'm going to scream." Lily actually loved the episode of Michael and Carly's show where he proposed, thought it was the most romantic thing she'd ever seen, but she couldn't take it right now. Not with her own love life in shambles.

Carly laughed, scrolling through the entries and finally deciding that the most recently recorded show was the one in question. "He wouldn't do that. I guess *Jeopardy!* it is. Maybe there's a hilarious answer or something. Who knows with that man? There could be a crazy personal injury lawyer commercial." She shrugged and settled against the couch, holding her wine glass by the bowl.

They watched the first segment of the show, paying close attention to the questions, the contestants, waiting for Alex Trebek to accidentally drop an F bomb or something, but nothing stood out. The show went to commercial, and the familiar patriotic music heard so often this time of year as part of political campaign ads played. As Lily was moving forward to grab the wine bottle to refill her glass, Ford came onscreen, leaning casually against an unfamiliar desk in an office she assumed was in Washington D.C. She stopped midway to the bottle, her hand in the air, eyes wide.

"Is this a joke? Does Michael really think we want to see a political ad?"

Carly looked uncomfortable. When it came down to it, Lily didn't know Michael that well, only what she'd learned through Carly and through spending time with them together. Maybe he had a mean streak or sadistic sense of humor that she didn't know about.

Ford's rich voice filled the room, and Lily's stomach clutched. With any hope, he wouldn't be re-elected, and she'd never have to see his face or hear that voice again. Her heart couldn't take it. Despite everything, she still wanted him, still loved him, still dreamed of being with him.

His handsome, serious face dominated her thoughts as he spoke. "My fellow Texans, it's been a difficult campaign this time around. Being your representative has been one of the greatest honors and privileges of my life. I've been proud to serve you during my first term, and I'd love nothing more than to return for another. I hope you'll join me at the polls this week and cast your votes for the candidates of your choice. Many of you have seen or heard the accusations that my opponent, Sam Coldwell, has leveled against both my campaign and me personally. He's told you that I can't understand family values because I'm not married, and then he questioned the authenticity of my engagement to Lily Ashton, a beautiful and intelligent woman. You may have seen her appearance on a local morning talk show, or at least read about it afterwards. He's taken her words out of context, has forced her private life into the public eye, and has minimized her personal tragedy, turning it into no more than a sound bite. All that is bad…." He looked directly into the camera, and Lily held her breath for a second. "But what I've done is worse. I've been told to focus on the campaign, to worry about winning the election. In doing that, I've hurt the woman I love. I'm coming to you today to share a message with you. I want your vote, but I'm no longer willing to compromise my personal beliefs to get it." He spread his hands. "It's that simple. I'm in love with Lily Ashton, and I want to marry her. You've seen pictures of her at her husband's funeral, you've seen her interviewed on television, and you've heard the rhetoric. It's meant to confuse you and skew your perception. The truth of the matter is this." The camera panned away enough to show both Ford and an American flag. "She is a true patriot, someone who has made the ultimate sacrifice for her country. She deserves better than this, and starting now, she's not a part of this narrative. I hope you'll vote for me, I truly do, but I won't answer any questions about Ms. Ashton, and I won't allow her name to be brought into my campaign again. I challenge Mr. Coldwell to do the same. Thank you, and God bless America."

The ad was paid for by Ford Richardson, not the Ford Richardson campaign, so he'd likely gone against the wishes of his advisory team and bought the time himself. There's no way they signed off on that message; they probably thought he was practically committing career suicide.

Lily sat in stunned silence, still not entirely certain of what she'd heard. Carly's mouth hung open until she recovered from her shock and stared at her, wide-eyed. "Oh. My. Gosh. If that's not enough for you, then I don't know what else he could do."

"I literally can't believe what we just saw." Lily set her glass on the table, hand shaking. "Why would he do that?"

"You wouldn't answer when he tried to reach you, so it looks like he got to you the best way he could. This is bananas!" Carly bounced in her excitement, a huge smile on her face.

"What should I do?" Lily's mind was racing as quickly as her heart.

"Um, you go to him and beg him to take you back. You've got a man who just made a very sincere, probably incredibly expensive, public apology. You hang on and you don't let go, that's what you do." She grabbed her by the forearms and shook dramatically. "This is like a fairy tale, Lily. I can't believe it!"

Carly fanned herself dramatically and fell back against the couch, the dreamy smile still on her face. She was right. Lily wanted Ford to man up and be the protector she'd dreamed of. She wanted him to put their relationship first and to show her that she was more important to him than anything else. Even after throwing up every obstacle she could between them, he'd found a way to get to her. He'd done everything she wanted, and he'd done it in grand fashion. It didn't matter who was wrong, who'd messed up, or what had happened. They were meant to be together, and he was definitely the one.

Chapter Twelve

Waiting the couple of days between Ford's televised apology and Election Day was sheer torture. She couldn't wait to hear his voice again, but a phone call wasn't enough. She wanted to reunite in person, to see Ford's face when she told him that she loved him, that she forgave him for everything, and that she wanted to be with him. It was the best way to be sure that she'd made the right decision, that he truly felt the same way. Lily could hardly sleep from the excitement and nerves, but with Carly, work, and Soldier On for distraction, she'd managed. After a morning jog, she found her poll location and ducked inside, hurrying to avoid any prying eyes. With any luck, hers wouldn't be one of the busier polling places where news crews ran their Election Day stories and she would get in, vote, and get out without notice.

The quiet lobby of the large city library where she'd be voting looked clear enough. She shuffled into the multipurpose room they'd designated for voters and gave her card to one of the line of elderly voting officials lining the table up front. She confirmed her address and winked at the older man with his eyebrows raised in recognition and silent question. With a fingertip to her lips, she hurried over to the first available voting machine. The computerized touch screen was separated by others in the row by plastic dividers for privacy, so much less exciting than the individual booths she'd seen in movies. When she was a kid, she'd envisioned closing herself in a curtained booth, marking her choices, maybe pulling a lever. Seeing Ford's name pop up on her Congressional choices was a rush, though, and she chose him, glad to send a vote his way.

After voting, she rushed across town to pick up her special print order and got ready for Election Night.

•••

Ford paced the length of the small room behind the stage, wondering how many other people in the same position had done so. They'd rented a ballroom in a local hotel for the Election Night results party, and revelers had filled the space as soon as the doors opened. The utilitarian, bland room was lined with folding chairs and tables, likely overflow from the event room. Fluorescent overhead lights buzzed, an errant candy wrapper crinkled under his step, and he walked on, back and forth. What an unremarkable room to wait for such remarkable news in. Since his apology video aired and nothing happened between him and Lily, he'd lost interest in whether he won or lost the election. Without Lily, with the final knowledge that he'd really lost her forever, nothing much mattered. He'd been so certain that a big apology, one where he admitted complete fault and begged for forgiveness, would be enough, that she'd come running back to him. When she didn't, when his calls remained unanswered, an emptiness replaced the hope he'd come to rely on. Without that hope, there was nothing to look forward to. There weren't any tricks up his sleeve. He was out of ideas. And now it was time to move on. Alone.

The door opened and closed with a quiet click. "Hey." Robert joined him, bearing a folder and a bottle of water. "The numbers are coming in, with almost all precincts reporting. We're waiting on a couple more before we know for sure. It's looking really good."

"Oh? That's awesome." He wanted to be excited, and he knew he owed it to his team to at least try to summon some enthusiasm for the campaign they'd worked so hard for. The best he could do was a weak smile and a nod of appreciation for the water. He took a seat by a small table and opened the folder Robert brought him.

"So, is it safe to assume that you haven't heard from Lily?" Robert pulled up a chair and took a seat by Ford. The votes were cast, and all that was left to do was wait. Robert could afford to be a friend and not a campaign advisor now.

The team had been much less angry than he'd feared after he filmed the spot and bought the airtime. They'd met the news with a resignation that told him they didn't expect much of anything from him after the way he'd mucked up the fiancée portion of their strategy. He supposed everything else had fallen apart so irreparably, they couldn't fault him for a last-ditch effort at scavenging what he could of his personal life. They'd grudgingly admitted that he probably hadn't made things any worse and that some voters might be moved by his sincerity. There was only one voter that he cared about, and she apparently wasn't moved.

"Nope, not a word. I guess that's it for us." He sipped from the water bottle. "I gave it my best shot, but it's not going to work out. Sometimes things are too far gone to fix."

He rubbed his hands together and bounced his knees, summoning the energy and enthusiasm he'd need to face the crowd waiting on the other side of the wall. Win or lose tonight, he had an obligation to the team, to the voters, and to the party guests to put his best face forward. His personal problems would still be around in the morning, and he could wallow in his misery then. Tonight he had to be professional and play the politician. People had given countless hours, incredible amounts of money, and their votes to get him where he was, and he had to repay them with enthusiasm. All he needed was a few more minutes alone to psych himself up, to get his signature charm ramped up enough to be a good host to his guests.

"Anything I need to know about the speeches?" He indicated the folder Robert had given him.

"Nope, they're both here, and they should be exactly as you expect. Everything should be perfect, but it wouldn't hurt to take one last look."

"Okay then." He halfheartedly flipped through the pages. He'd been over both speeches so carefully already, and they looked fine. He didn't have the energy to waste on more proofing. Checking the time, he stood. "Should be about time, don't you think?"

"Yeah, let me go see if we have an answer yet." Robert left him alone with the speeches and his thoughts.

In moments, Ford would know if he'd be making or receiving a concession call to Sam Coldwell. Whatever the result, the last thing he wanted to do was talk to that guy. Coldwell had been at the source of all his problems lately, and he wasn't ready to forgive and forget. Politics or not, he'd done his level best to destroy his and Lily's personal lives. As much as Ford had been able to accept his fault in the matter, much of it would never have come about without Coldwell's actions. He'd keep it quick and cordial, possibly letting his tone tell Mr. Coldwell just what he thought of his campaign tactics, whichever way the vote fell.

Robert burst back through the door with a huge grin on his face, fists in the air victoriously. "Looks like you'll be getting a phone call soon!"

The rest of the team followed, all smiles, the tension of the last week gone in the face of their triumph. For tonight, at least, the difficulties would be forgotten in the thrill of victory. So the results were in, and Ford was going back to D.C. Sam Coldwell had thrown everything he had at their campaign, but they still won, and it felt pretty good. Another term on his political resume for him, another big win for the campaign advisors. Maybe they could pull together when it was time to aim for the governor's mansion. It would've been better if Lily were there to share the moment, but this was as good as it was going to get. He accepted their hugs, handshakes, and congratulations, thanked them each personally for their stellar work, and paced the room, waiting for the phone to ring.

When it did, a hush fell over the group and Ford counted to three before answering, steadying his breath and mentally preparing himself to speak to the enemy. "Hello."

"Mr. Richardson? It's Sam Coldwell. I'm calling to congratulate you on your victory. You fought a good fight, you ran a clean campaign, and you deserve the win. I'm proud to have you represent my interests in Washington. Congratulations, sir." The voice on the other end of the line was clear and strong, and Ford knew he must be steeling himself against an attack, waiting for Ford to go off on him. As professionals, of course they were expected to gloss over all the personal animosity between them. They'd had trouble keeping things professional during the campaign, though, and anything could happen.

He'd lost the only thing he truly cared about, and whatever he might have thought about Sam Coldwell, it didn't matter now. The fight had gone out of him when Lily hadn't come back. Coldwell had started it, but Ford could've saved his relationship if only he'd been man enough. "Thank you, sir. I appreciate your confidence." He ended the call and faced his team. The relief on their faces that he hadn't caused another scandal by calling Coldwell out was unmistakable.

Going off on the man wouldn't make him feel better, and it would make him look horrible. There was nothing left to do besides address the crowd and party the night away like he was elated with the victory. His years in politics had given him enough practice, so he'd be able to mingle all night, laugh at jokes, and share amusing anecdotes. He could collapse and be miserable later, when he was home. Alone.

"All right, then. We have a full house out there, and everybody is ready to hear the results. Let's give the people what they want." He painted the smile on his face and followed his team into the ballroom.

Before they reached the end of the short hall leading to the door, he could hear the crowd. Loud music was playing, people were laughing and chatting, and dishes clinked. With a deep breath, he pushed open the door and beamed at the crowd as the spotlight followed him bounding up the stairs of the stage. He reached the podium and waved, smiling for a moment while the music played, and waited for a break in the noise. The room was full of people wearing the traditional cheesy political accessories everyone associated with Election Night parties: buttons; red, white, and blue top hats; zany sunglasses and vests; the whole nine yards. Signs with his name and slogans were held by revelers, and a disco ball threw splashes of light bathed in red and white around the room. He'd been here before, but it was still a thrill to know that in a few moments the room would erupt with excitement when he made his announcement. Bathing in the anticipation of sharing the news, knowing it would be met with such happiness, cheered him. He'd focus on making his next term worth the voters' confidence, stop dwelling on things he couldn't control.

Finally the music died down and the spotlight was firmly on the podium. A couple hundred pairs of eyes were trained on the stage, and everyone held their collective breath. He leaned down to reach the microphone and grinned, savoring the moment.

"I just received a phone call from Sam Coldwell congratulating me on winning this election. We did it!" The crowd went wild, cheering and clapping. Balloons and fat strips of silver confetti dropped from the ceiling, flooding the room and ramping up the excitement tenfold. Ford took a moment to soak it all in. It was so easy to forget that he wasn't the only one invested in the campaign, and to share the excitement with a roomful of ecstatic people was a rush. He'd worried about having to force his enthusiasm, but he was swept up in the pure energy of the crowd. "Looks like you're stuck with me for a few more years. This campaign was hard fought and hard won, and I couldn't have done any of it without my amazing team of advisors…" He held out his arm to indicate the team of seven and clapped for them, blowing a two-handed kiss in their direction. "And the interns, the volunteers, the voters, and the donors. You have no idea how much your support, your hard work, your faith in me, and of course, your campaign donations, mean to me." The crowd laughed and he continued. "Thank you from the bottom of my heart. I am honored to be your representative, and I will do my best to earn your trust in my next term. Enough talk, let's party!"

The music started again, drowning out the crowd's loud shouts, and he strode across the stage, smiling and waving at the crowd. The signs bobbing amongst the guests blurred into one another, except for one. He stopped dead in his tracks, physically unable to move for a moment as his mind made sense of the words he was reading. In the middle of a sea of faces, a single sign stood out. In bold white letters against a black background, the message was clear: I LOVE YOU, FORD.

Lily.

Here.

Love?

Their eyes met, and everything faded into the background. Gone were the flashing lights, the loud music, the pulsing crowd. Only the two of them, and they couldn't get to each other fast enough. He cut through the crowd, ignoring the extended hands, congratulations, and pats on the back as he made a beeline to Lily. She waited, radiant and brilliant, for him in the crowd until he finally reached her and swept her into his arms. Holding her tight, twirling once on the dance floor, and vaguely registering that the sign she'd held hit his leg as she let it fall to the floor, he held her. Her scent surrounded him as he breathed her in, setting her down gently but unwilling to let her go. With a gentle hand at her jaw, he tipped her face up until their lips met and kissed her. The kiss asked and answered every question, settled every debt, told them everything they needed to know. The kiss sealed their future and forgave their past. The kiss made every moment of heartbreak fall away, forgotten in the moment.

Lily pressed her cheek to Ford's and murmured into his ear. "I saw your video. I think it would've been cheaper to hire a skywriter." She laughed, the warmth of her breath on his earlobe sending a shiver down his back.

"You wouldn't take my calls. Desperate times call for desperate measures." He shrugged, letting the tension, misery, and uncertainty fall away with the light joke. With her in his arms, every dark moment was forgotten.

She quirked an eyebrow. "Desperate? In that case, I think I'm flattered."

Ford wrapped his arms around her waist in a loose circle, falling into their familiar rhythm. "You should be. I almost never make expensive apology videos for women."

With a playful swat on his arm, she laughed. "Almost never?"

"Well, I never want to have to do it again." He'd never let her go again.

"You won't have to." Her brown eyes caught the dancing light of the ballroom, holding his future and all its possibilities.

"I would do anything for you. Anything."

"I know you would. I didn't realize it before, but I do now."

His mind went to the Tiffany box holding her engagement ring sitting on a shelf in his closet. "Will you come home with me tonight?"

A delightfully wicked grin spread across her lips, and she swiveled closer to him, lowering her eyes. "Hmm. You move quickly. What did you have in mind?"

"I want to propose to you."

The playfulness disappeared as she grew still in his arms. Had he jumped the gun? "Even after everything that's happened?"

The breath rushed out, relief filling his chest. "Yes, of course after everything. Because of everything. You're the love of my life, Lily, and I don't want to wake up another morning without knowing you'll be my wife."

"Yes, I will."

"Go home with me tonight, or be my wife?" He knew the answer, but there could be no doubt between them. Never again would he hold back, withholding affection or devotion to avoid getting hurt. He would make sure Lily knew the love of a man who believed in her, cherished her, and would do anything for her.

"Both."

"This is seriously the best night of my entire life. I love you, and I'll spend the rest of our lives making you glad you said yes."

More from This Author
(From *The Confection Connection* by Monica Tillery)

Carly Piper hung up the phone and blew out an aggravated breath. Last week, a refrigerator went out, costing her several hundred dollars she couldn't exactly spare, and now an oven? Her bakery, Caketopia, couldn't do without it, and with the biggest pitch of her life happening in less than an hour, she didn't have the time to deal with it. With a quick roll of her neck and shoulders, she mentally tallied the extra time it would take to handle the pitch without an assistant. Speaking of, her employee's heels clacked on the tile floor, announcing her imminent arrival. How Layla Jameson managed to work in those shoes confounded Carly.

"Hey, I was just about to find you. I've got a repair guy coming for the oven, so I need you to stay here. I'll have to go on the pitch alone." Carly untied her apron and hung it on a hook.

"Are you sure? That's a lot of stuff to carry." Layla towered over Carly, especially in those ridiculous shoes. "It'll be crowded, and you might have to make more than one trip. With nobody there to help you—"

"I don't see any way around it. If we don't get this stupid oven fixed, we'll fall behind on this week's orders. With my luck, the other one will probably go out, too."

Layla laughed, then stopped when she saw that Carly wasn't joking. Between the constant repairs, the economy, and competition, Caketopia struggled to remain successful. Getting this job could mean the beginning of a new era for Carly and her business. Sure, it would be easier to concentrate on the pitch if Layla went with her, but she was a professional. She could win over the celebrity couple planning their wedding without help. She had to.

"All right," Layla said. "I'll go load the van, at least. You just get ready, and I'll see you outside."

Carly packed her bag with binders that held photos of her work, Caketopia information she could leave with the couple, and a contract ready for them to sign if things went her way. After kicking off her rubber clogs, she slipped her feet into much less comfortable but infinitely more flattering shoes before swiping fresh gloss across her lips and heading out to the van. Hopefully the desperation would be replaced by her usual calm professionalism by the time she arrived at the swanky uptown hotel.

A blast of warm air greeted her as she crossed the parking lot to her refrigerated van. Layla, ever the mind-reader, had already turned the van on, ensuring that it would be nice and cool for the drive to the hotel. There, Carly would either secure the biggest job of her career, guaranteeing more business than she could dream of, or come back to the same old thing, paying bills she could scarcely afford. Before she second-guessed herself any more, Carly opened the door and slid in, noting with satisfaction that she could at least afford the new van. Now she didn't have to worry about snagging her clothes on the ragged vinyl of her old delivery vehicle. The smooth new seats and cold air conditioning reminded her of how far she'd already come.

She rolled down the window. "Wish me luck!" What she meant was more like, *Cross your fingers and toes because getting this job means we'll be set from now on*, but she gave Layla a bright smile.

"Knock 'em dead, boss," Layla said with a little wave as she squinted in the sunlight.

Carly pulled out of the parking lot and navigated the van through Dallas traffic to Central Expressway, and started to relax as the city flew past. She was an accomplished professional, an award winner in her field, and the chance to make the cakes for a high-profile celebrity wedding should feel exciting. It shouldn't feel like she was heading for the trial of her life. Being prepared always boosted her confidence, so she reviewed her spiel, which, after delivering it for so many years, she could recite in her sleep. Now all she had to do was show up and wow the client. No problem, right?

Before long, she was dodging paparazzi and curious onlookers as she turned toward the back of the hotel. Celebrities visiting Dallas often stayed at the hot spot, and the news must be out that country music superstar Rusty Grainger and his notoriously quirky fiancée, actress Sequoia Rivers were on site. At the service entrance, Carly parked the van and got to work stacking her signature lavender bakery boxes into neat rows on a dolly. She hoisted her oversized canvas bag over her shoulder and trekked through the parking garage to the door. Once inside, Carly took in the hotel's lush, almost bacchanalian atmosphere with wide eyes and an appreciation for the stunning attention to detail. From the gleaming black marble floors to the plush burgundy brocade on the walls, the place screamed elegant debauchery. She parked the dolly and fished a card out of her pocket to check the suite name once more before the elevator arrived.

Ensconced in the tiny decadent space, she concentrated on her breathing, reminding herself that her work was top-notch. Best to focus on the positive and try to forget how badly she needed the business. As the elevator slowed, she adjusted her bag on her shoulder and held her head high. The doors whooshed open, and silence greeted her. Silence, a near empty hallway, and Michael Welch.

He whistled innocently as she rolled her eyes. Without so much as flinching under her withering gaze, he brushed past her into the elevator. "Going up, Carly?"

He tapped the "close door" button and stood an inch away from her. Of course *he* would be here. Why hadn't she anticipated that?

She'd met Michael Welch three years ago when they were rival contestants on the Cuisine Network's popular reality competition show *Sugar Shock*, where hopeful bakers battled to create exciting cakes and pastries and complete ridiculous challenges. His charisma, charm, and talent—combined with thick brown hair, a chiseled jaw, and piercing green eyes—made it hard for Carly to reconcile her attraction to him with her irritation. Everyone—show personnel, other contestants, the viewers—seemed to love him, but everything he did rubbed Carly the wrong way. He was almost too good-looking and too personable.

For Carly, the two high points of the *Sugar Shock* experience came on the day she found out she'd been accepted for that season and the day she was voted off and could get away from Michael. Spending months with him on set hadn't endeared him to her, but he'd somehow managed to pull her under his magnetic spell. They'd shared a confusing and stupid kiss—moments before the challenge that sealed her fate, of course. No matter how much he protested and pleaded innocence, he knew what he was doing. She was thrown off her game and sent home, while he went on to compete in the final competition and won the whole thing. She wasn't even disappointed to be eliminated so close to the end, since it was such a relief to finally be rid of him.

Even though it was clear she wasn't cut out for cutthroat TV competitions, the experience and recognition that had come with the show brought new opportunities. Carly could finally open her own shop, where she happily spent her days creating beautiful confections to celebrate the most important days of her clients' lives. The work was invigorating and satisfying, everything she'd ever wanted.

They reached their floor, and Carly set her mind to ignore the memories evoked by his too-familiar cinnamon-chocolate scent.

"Nervous, cupcake?"

"Of course."

"Why? Because every hoity-toity bakery from here to Fort Worth is competing for the same job? Because you've suddenly decided that your cakes aren't fancy enough for primetime? Or is it because you finally get to see me again after all these years?" He waggled his eyebrows suggestively, and the tension she'd been carrying around in her shoulders all day disappeared in a quick burst of laughter.

"Oh, yeah, that's it." She'd hoped for confident sarcasm, but heard a prim quality in her voice that made her cringe. Maybe breathing the same air would somehow help his confidence rub off on her. She ignored how warm her cheeks felt and gripped the handle of her bag.

"Come on. We got this." There was no "we," but she knew if she reminded him of that, he'd have a snappy comeback that would make her feel like a fool. He pulled his signature black skullcap tight over his head, his green eyes glinting with enthusiasm. Without asking, he commandeered her dolly and pulled it out of the elevator. "Let's roll."

"Didn't you bring samples or anything? Are you planning to win the couple over on charm alone?"

"I brought an assistant from my shop with me today, and she has my things. You happened to catch me on my way back upstairs from checking out the amenities. Don't worry about my pitch."

The view was just as good both coming and going, and she hated herself for noticing. Michael shot her one last look over his shoulder before heading down the hall, making her wonder if she'd broadcasted her thoughts.

Carly spent the short walk drawing from his confidence and trying to project some semblance of her own. Michael stopped outside the door, rapped twice, and stepped back. A wispy blonde dressed head to toe in black, holding a clipboard, and barking orders into a walkie-talkie answered.

"Names and business?" The blonde didn't look up as Carly and Michael each provided their information. "I have Michael Welch, and I have Caketopia. So which is it?"

"They're two separate businesses. Caketopia is mine, and The Clubhouse is his." Carly tried to see the listings on the page as the woman went through them again.

"Okay, well, we have one appointment left, and it's for Michael Welch of Caketopia. Who wants it?"

Carly's heart sank as she realized what had happened. She needed the job—her future nearly depended on it—but not if it meant pushing a legitimate competitor out of the way to get it. "We have two separate bakeries, so we both want it."

"You can both go in if you share the appointment. The rest of the day is booked."

Michael patted Carly on the shoulder. "Come on. We'll split the time and explain what happened when we get in there."

"Are you sure?"

"Yep. Let's do this. The worst that can happen is neither one of us gets the job. We've got to at least try."

Michael nodded to the blonde woman, and she spoke into her walkie-talkie about the change of plans.

Carly was immediately glad that she'd let Michael talk her into sharing the appointment. The air was charged with excitement and possibility. The huge entourage necessary to staff the venture swirled around a common spot in the middle of the room, rushing around, chattering into phones, and checking clipboards. One of the country's most famous couples sat at an elaborately carved wooden table, in absurdly oversized purple velvet chairs, as though they were holding court.

As Carly looked around, taking everything in and mentally rehearsing her spiel, Michael strode through the crowd and headed straight to Rusty's table. He was in his element, sure of his abilities and that he was right where he belonged. That confidence was half the reason he'd won the reality show. His creative and fearless designs explained the rest.

Rusty Grainger, the groom, stood, and his eyes lit up with recognition.

"You're Michael Welch," he exclaimed. His head swiveled from one to the other. "And you're Carly Piper, from that show! What was it called, babe?" He turned to his fiancée, who was decidedly less impressed. Not surprising, given her reputation. Sequoia Rivers was a hugely famous movie star known more for her quirky new age habits than for her glitzy roles. She appeared to delight in not caring what or who was hot, and she wasn't likely to be drawn in by Michael's swagger or impressed by pseudo-famous bakers.

"*Sugar Shock*." She stopped short of rolling her eyes.

"You're hired, man." Rusty thrust his hand out, and Michael grabbed it, shaking heartily as they voiced their mutual admiration for one another. A short blonde bearing a dolly stacked with Michael's signature red-and-black bakery boxes arrived and silently unloaded his materials.

"Not so fast, honey. Let's at least taste the cakes first. Plus, I don't know if I want some chocolate-jalapeño cake shaped like an armadillo or something at our wedding." Fortunately, Carly was prepared to show both her classic, traditional designs as well as a few she'd created to reflect Sequoia's earthy, natural sensibilities.

Carly went to work organizing her own samples and portfolios, bolstered by Sequoia's obvious lack of enthusiasm for Michael. Customers appreciated Carly's elegant style, her ability to put fresh twists on classic design, and her impeccable attention to detail. She wasn't flashy, and she definitely wasn't famous, but she had built a name for herself. A reputation built on exquisite quality, cake by cake.

She lined up plates with small hand-lettered placards that labeled each flavor. She gave Rusty and Sequoia each a fork, then set up a binder full of cake photos for each of them. Michael did the same with the wilder flavors from his own shop. Carly then launched into her pitch. Experience had taught her that a groom's enthusiasm means nothing if the bride isn't interested. The bride's opinion is what really matters, when it comes down to it.

"These are the most popular flavors at Caketopia, but I would be delighted to work with you if there's something you want that you don't see here." She waved her hand over samples of her classic white chocolate cake and watched as they tasted bites of coconut, lemon, and Italian crème cake. "Many brides can't or don't want to choose just one, so we can do the layers in different flavors. We can also create something beautiful by mixing and matching frosting flavors and choosing different fresh fruits to complement your choices."

"If you want something a little less run of the mill, try these." Michael pushed his Mexican chocolate, red velvet, gingerbread, and toasted almond samples forward. "The Clubhouse offers frostings that are a bit more unique as well. Let's see, we've got Kahlua, mocha, chocolate peanut butter, and hazelnut. I can do more traditional choices as well."

Rusty tried Michael's cakes, obviously savoring each bite as he made appreciative noises, and Sequoia looked as though she were ready to slap somebody. It looked as though she would turn them both down just to get Michael away from the table.

"Sequoia, what do you have in mind for your wedding cake?" Carly took a chance, hoping that Sequoia was like most brides and could be diverted when given the chance to wax poetic about her big day. She wasn't disappointed.

Sequoia's face took on the dreamy look Carly had seen on countless brides before her. "I want it to be elegant, but sweet, you know? I want it to be special, unique, and even glamorous. If people saw it and thought of a fairy tale, that would be perfect." Mentally shelving the quirky nature-inspired designs she'd prepared, Carly nodded. She'd expected to hear that Sequoia dreamt of an environmentally responsible wedding, maybe something spiritual or nature-inspired. An elegant fairy tale was the last thing Carly expected, but it was absolutely something she could deliver.

"And I can do that. We can work together to create something that has never been done before, something uniquely you. I want you to look at the portfolio, but your cake isn't in here because it hasn't been designed yet. It'll be one of a kind, just like you."

"Ooh, I like the sound of that." Sequoia's eyes sparkled, and Carly forged ahead to close the deal, hoping that Michael would realize what was happening and keep his mouth closed. While Carly struggled to start her own business, Michael had already published a cookbook and shot a pilot. It wasn't picked up, and he eventually returned to Dallas to open his own bakery, but from what she could tell, he was an instant success. His moderate fame from *Sugar Shock* and the cookbook translated into big business back home.

"Maybe these are a little too out-there for your wedding cake." Carly indicated Michael's more daring flavor samples. "But people love something new and exotic for a groom's cake, and I'd be more than happy to work with you to create that."

"We can do something fancy and elegant for the wedding cake, and Rusty can do whatever crazy combination he wants for the groom's cake? That sounds perfect to me!" The bride clasped her hands together and nodded decisively. "What do you think, honey?"

"What?" Her groom looked up from the portfolio, his mouth full of gingerbread cake. "Whatever you want, baby doll."

"Great, then you two are hired. When can we get started?" Sequoia pressed her hands together on her lap and bobbed a little in her seat, clearly excited by the possibilities.

Carly's delight at being hired on the spot for such a huge job fizzled when she realized what Sequoia was saying. She and Michael weren't a package deal. They didn't work together, she didn't want to work together, and she didn't want him anywhere near this wedding. Determined not to freak out, she focused on retaining her professional persona. "On a job this size, you'll be my first priority. Simply let me know when you're available, and my staff and I will be there. I want to make sure everything is perfect for your big day." She pulled a manila folder from her bag and passed it to Sequoia. "If you would review and sign the agreement, we'll get the process started."

Michael looked like he wanted to interject, but Carly shot him a look and shook her head the tiniest bit. She would offer him something to get him to concede later on, anything he wanted, so she could have the account. There was no way he needed the work as badly as she did. Besides, if the bride wasn't on board, he had no chance of getting the job anyway.

Sequoia's pen hovered over the agreement. "I can't wait to get started. I want to do the cake, maybe a dessert bar, probably something for the bridesmaids' luncheon. I'm so glad we found you. I hadn't thought about trying to find a couple to work on the cakes, but here you are. It feels right, you know? Like it's meant to be. It's going to be so great!"

"You mean me and him?" Carly waggled a thumb between herself and Michael.

Sequoia's brow furrowed in confusion. Obviously the message that two companies were pitching during the same appointment hadn't reached her. "Are you two not together?"

Michael closed the distance between them and slung an arm over Carly's shoulder before pressing a kiss to her temple. She ignored the way heat shot through her at the casual contact, and forced herself to focus on the job instead of remembering the last time his lips had touched hers. His voice rolled over her, the words sounding so natural she almost believed them herself. "Oh no, we are definitely together. We just try to keep things professional when we go out on a job. You must be very perceptive to pick up on our relationship."

Sequoia visibly relaxed and looked pleased with his reply, scrawling her signature on the agreement as she spoke. "I guess when you're in love, you can see it in others as well. I want to surround our union with love and light, and I think it's important that the dessert that represents our marriage is baked with love, not infused with negative emotions or loneliness."

"Oh, sure. I think you're absolutely right." Michael was close enough that Carly could feel his warm breath against her cheek, and an unwelcome shiver skipped down her spine. What were they getting themselves into?

Sequoia was well known for her quirky beliefs and her odd proclivities. She'd joined Rusty on tour and had cleared entire rooms when she felt the staff projected negativity. It wasn't unusual for her to rearrange furniture or nix decorations if she thought a room's energy flow was off. But pretending to be a couple was a bit much. Carly pasted a pleasant smile on her face and gazed at Michael with adoration while they packed up their samples. As they wound through the crowd, she maintained the ruse, even going so far as to accept a playful pat on her rear without so much as flinching.

Once in the hall, with the door safely closed behind them, Carly put some distance between them and snapped. "What the hell were you thinking?"

To her consternation, he laughed. "I was thinking that we should do whatever it takes to get the job. Why is the thought of pretending to be with me so disgusting?"

"Is everything a joke to you?" He'd acted the same way on *Sugar Shock*, and it still annoyed her.

"Of course not, but I don't see the harm in going along with this one little thing if it means we get the job."

"If *we* get the job? *We* don't work together, Michael."

"Looks like we do now, cupcake, unless you want to go back in there and tell them they need to find someone else. I don't know if you noticed, but Sequoia seems to have made up her mind that she needs a couple in love to work on her wedding cakes. Maybe you don't care about the exposure, but I do. This could lead to major work in the future, and if it means pretending that we're together, that's a small price to pay."

"But it's lying." Hearing it out loud made Carly realize how weak her excuse sounded.

"So don't lie. All you have to do is pretend you don't cringe at the sight of me, and we'll be fine. This is one job, and then we can go back to never seeing each other again. It's not like Sequoia's going to ask if we want to double date with her and Rusty. Just follow my lead and relax. I've got this covered." His green eyes twinkled with amusement. Once again he was completely at ease while she was up in arms.

She put up her hands in surrender. "Fine. I'll go along with it, but only in front of them. Don't get any ideas."

Michael stepped closer, invading her space, reminding her of that one idiotic kiss they'd shared. As he tucked a tendril of hair behind her ear, he murmured, "What makes you think I'd get any ideas?"

"I don't know. Just don't." She walked toward the elevator, leaving him standing alone with that cocky smirk on his face. She hated that he still rattled her. Hated more that her heart raced as his voice wound its way around her like a warm breeze.

Praise for *The Confection Connection*:

" ... she creates great characters that you can't help but fall for."—4.5 stars, Up All Night, Read All Day

"*The Confection Connection* ... flows easily, leaving you feeling warm and cozy throughout. The characters are well developed, believable and the attraction between the two is intense and yet modest."—Eat Sleep Read Review

"When two people (who) think they hate each other are forced to work together and then fall in love, it makes for a sweet, sultry romance."—4 stars, Ebooks Galore Reviews

"If you watch a lot of cooking shows on TV, put down the remote and pick up this book, especially when something boring is on, i.e. a recipe not involving sugar or butter."—Lyra's Musings

"*The Confection Connection* brings together two former rivals who realize that there is a fine line between love and hate, and creates a story that is sugary sweet."—Night Owl Reviews

For more books by Monica Tillery, check out:

A Sweet Deal

Praise for *A Sweet Deal*:

"Monica's characters make you want to cheer for them and hug them tight when their hearts break. The storylines are based on real life . . . . sex and candy, what more could a girl want? This is a quick read for those summer days by the pool, catching some rays."—Confessions of a Book Lovin' Junkie, 5 stars

"Ms. Tillery gives us a twist with this sweet tale set in the industry of confections. The arc of the story flows well and the limited amount of characters makes this a quick and easy read. *A Sweet Deal* is a great romantic love story that does see its up and downs as it shows a creative way to portray a classic love story."—Julie Caicco, *InD Tale Magazine*

Adam's Ambition

Praise for *Adam's Ambition*:

"I recommend this read for every fan of romance. It was sweet, sensual, passionate, heart-stopping and gave me the perfect 'home is where the heart is' feeling I love so much!"—Contemporary Romance Reviews

Kiss Me, Katie

Praise for Kiss Me, Katie:

"Sassy and sexy, *Kiss Me, Katie* is a charming debut with larger than life characters and lots of sizzle!"—Jane Porter, RITA finalist and author of Lifetime movie *Flirting With Forty*

"A delightful novella romance. Tales of music stars finding love will adore Tillery's first book and will sigh with a smile at the end."—*In D'Tale Magazine*

"*Kiss Me, Katie* is a heartwarming love story with the music scene at its core. Strong, well-developed characters along with a great plot makes you feel like you're in the audience at one of their sold-out concerts. Sit back and enjoy the show. You'll be glad you did!"—Romance Junkies

In the mood for more Crimson Romance?
Check out *Core Attraction by Ashlinn Craven*
at *CrimsonRomance.com*.